YELLOW

YELLOW

a novel

oOo

Amy Pence

Red Hen Press | *Pasadena, CA*

Book design by Mark E. Cull
Interior Illustrations: Teah Charkawi

Library of Congress Cataloging-in-Publication Data

Names: Pence, Amy author
Title: Yellow : a novel / Amy Pence.
Description: First edition. | Pasadena, CA: Red Hen Press, 2026.
Identifiers: LCCN 2025034186 (print) | LCCN 2025034187 (ebook) |
ISBN 9781636284767 paperback | ISBN 9781636284781 library binding |
ISBN 9781636284774 ebook
Subjects: LCGFT: Novels | Fiction
Classification: LCC PS3616.E528 Y45 2026 (print) | LCC PS3616.E528 (ebook)
LC record available at https://lccn.loc.gov/2025034186
LC ebook record available at https://lccn.loc.gov/2025034187

The National Endowment for the Arts, the Los Angeles County Arts Commission, the Ahmanson Foundation, the Dwight Stuart Youth Fund, the Max Factor Family Foundation, the Pasadena Tournament of Roses Foundation, the Pasadena Arts & Culture Commission and the City of Pasadena Cultural Affairs Division, the City of Los Angeles Department of Cultural Affairs, the Audrey & Sydney Irmas Charitable Foundation, the Kinder Morgan Foundation, the Meta & George Rosenberg Foundation, the Albert and Elaine Borchard Foundation, the Adams Family Foundation, the Riordan Foundation, Amazon Literary Partnership, the Sam Francis Foundation, and the Mara W. Breech Foundation partially support Red Hen Press.

First Edition
Published by Red Hen Press
www.redhen.org

For my friend, Katy Silliman

oOo

You see, I want a lot.
Maybe I want it all.
The darkness of each endless fall,
The shimmering light of each ascent.

—Rainer Maria Rilke

Prologue

In the half-shadows of the lake, what can be seen?

The eye that looks back at the boy standing on the sandbar, bending to the crystal-flecked silt, his hair catching the sun.

The girl paralyzed with fear, caught by the hands that hold her, thumbs pressing into her neck's pearl.

The man wearing aviator frames, mirrored, the want of him a gaping hole. The man looks at the boy gazing into the water and instead sees a brilliance. Sees a grown man walking on water, such a sight that he drops his hands: how had the boy become the man coming toward him so swiftly?

He lets go—would not, could not murder another girl, but swims away as the boy peers absently from the sparkling silt and sees his sister. She stands frozen. The white body of the man like a water snake gliding away.

There were three, then there were two, and then there was one.

PART I

oooOoooo

It appeared overnight in our backyard, behind the pyracantha, between the plum and the black gum trees. Looking like a puffed mouse, an octopus head, or the great brain on the cartoon character Gazoo. It was all yellow.

Lighter than air or maybe filling with a kind of air. We were one and the same, but I didn't know it yet.

oooоOoooo

It was the summer of 1973. Summer of the Watergate hearings. You're thinking I'll say something about hippies, Kent State, or the Manson killings. But I was twelve, stuck in the incipient present, the past merely the past. I'd just awakened to what was beyond my own house, beyond my chaotic family. It was the summer that I learned that a president could lie. The summer of breaking and entering.

My innocence felt rubbed—the way the plush of flesh at the tops of my thighs would rub against each other.

Just as heat gathered during the day, then unwound at night, everything so new: the *V* of the just-opening flower between my thighs, the tender yellow plume of matter in my backyard.

oooo0oooo

1973 Timeline

February 12: American prisoners of war released from Vietnam

March 23: Watergate scandal: Watergate burglar James W. McCord admits he and other defendants had been pressured to remain silent

March 29: Last American soldier leaves Vietnam

April 3: First handheld cellular phone
call is made by Martin Cooper
in New York City

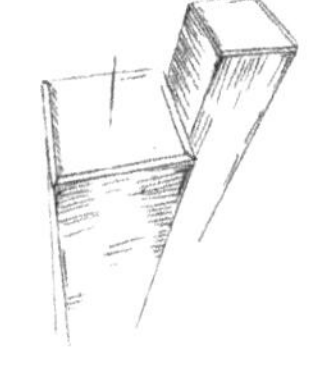

April 4: World Trade Center opens

April 6: Pioneer 11 is launched to study the solar

system

April 30: Watergate scandal: Nixon fires White House Counsel John Dean

May 17: Watergate scandal televised hearings begin in the US Senate

May 30: Unusual slime mold discovered in suburban backyard

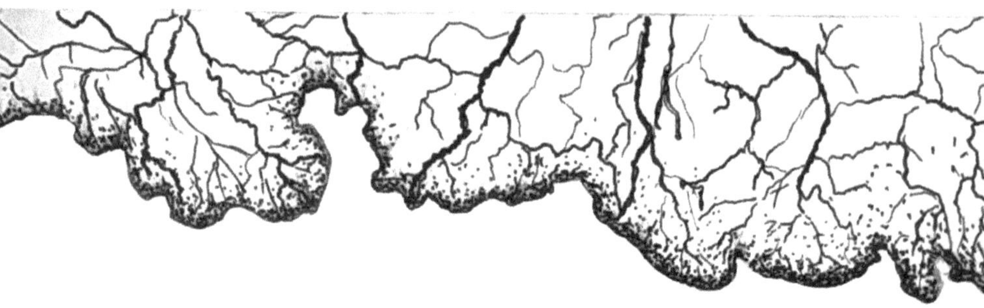

oooo0oooo

Let's say I live in Maine or on an island off the coast of Washington state. Anything but the plain truth: Metairie, Louisiana—a suburb of New Orleans surrounded by humped levees, those buried giant earthworms designed to protect us from water.

My name could be Harriet or June. I'd try out Jill, but I've known too many—their faces blurring with time—so truth is, I'm Eliza.

By my senior year, I would be called Z, but that's the future, and if nothing else, the yellow thing that billowed into a full-grown fist taught me this: the field of the present is an immensity.

oooo0oooo

I was bathed in green that summer, found the harbor of my backyard where I went to escape my mother's smothered rage and my father's drinking. Maybe everyone in the '70s lived in this twilight of depression and anger. The suburbia it imposed on us: we were children loosened in the dusk to reenact in rough games of hide and seek our parents' hopes and fears.

I tended to my aloneness, my friends' parties too packed with muddled emotion by midnight. Girls turned against each other one by one until everyone was rage-crying and misunderstood. Once you turned down a few invitations, the girls quit asking. I suppose you'd call me developmentally delayed. I was small with no breasts—I was a girl-boy or a boy-girl, not yet who I would become, and so I roamed my house at night feeling the world wasn't what it intended to be.

Shadows loomed into the house, frail markings of vast possibilities, of dimensions that no one could yet inhabit. A tone came with it and a taste. Like a wind rustling under your just-emergent wings, your tongue finding the ridges in your mouth, dreams of dripping honey.

oooo0oooo

The yellow blob had moved. I noticed it one dawn morning as my family slept inside the house. I'd gone barefoot outside wearing one of my dad's old T-shirts while it was still cool. So much fruit had fallen, and the bruised leaves wrinkled in a large pile under the plum tree. The blob had emerged the first time I saw it nearest a log ridged with those clown ear mushrooms. But now it was almost a foot further, looking plumper and quivering. A trail of what looked like snot behind it. I went towards it and the cells of my body clicked, both a longing and a calibration. We were both sensate. Without knowing the words for it, that is what I knew.

oooоOoooo

The *backyard blob*, as *The New York Times* reported, appeared in late May, though the story didn't run until August 6, 1973.

Never encountered before, the local botanist guessed it was a *fuligo, a compound of spores that group into a large protoplasm that feeds on bacteria and is usually seen in a yellow pulsating form.*

After isolation, the *scientists determined that the backyard blob is now dead and probably will not return.*

They were guessing, these scientists, assuring the public, but also puzzled about an organism that evaded their classification.

oooo Ooooo

The Watergate hearings were on all the time. My mother kept the small television on in the kitchen near the Formica table with its green pebbled surface. The TV in the living room was tuned to cartoons for the twins: *Speed Racer* and *Johnny Quest*. The twins, still in their Batman pajamas, held their cereal bowls right up to their elfin chins, their eyes owled in the colorful light dancing in the room.

My two older sisters yelled at each other in our shared bedroom, hurling hairbrushes at each other or mashing Juicy Fruit gum between their teeth. They were both swimmers and spent most of the summer at the pool, their hair going chlorine green, their rapt blue eyes often hovering over my small frame, asking me to do things for them.

Where did you come from anyway? Cheryl once said to me.

Mailman, Janice snickered back.

My twin bed formed the bottom of the *J* beneath Janice's bed with Cheryl's above her in the room. I felt exposed and hurried outside and away from everyone whenever I could.

Why don't you go to the pool with the girls? my mother asked of my retreating back more than once, but I didn't have to answer. I'd never taken to water from the beginning. I've always been smaller than anyone else my age. Rather than float, it's as if my body wanted to sink like a stone to the bottom of the pool.

Stones I loved and the feel of bark under my palms. I liked looking at the lichen in rocks. A trail weaved behind our clotted suburbia enroute to the levees, and I explored every turn. We were one of the poorest families in our parish neighborhood though not the largest. Like most Catholic kids, we went to school at St. Catherine until high school started in eighth grade. My mother was harried as she rounded us up for Mass on Sundays, and my father often opted out. We'd come home to see him pulling the tab on his first beer in front of the TV, tuned to the Saints.

I could get lost in that poor patch of wood, and I thought no one would find me. I couldn't sleep most nights and wandered through our narrow two-story house amid my family's breathing. My father's spluttering snores, my brothers like small puppies whimpering in the dark.

oooOoooo

Watergate Timeline

May 19, 1973: Independent special prosecutor Archibald Cox appointed to oversee investigation into possible presidential impropriety

June 3, 1973: John Dean tells Watergate investigators that he has discussed the cover-up with Nixon at least thirty-five times

July 13, 1973: Alexander Butterfield, former presidential appointments secretary, reveals all conversations and phone calls in Nixon's office have been taped since 1971

July 18, 1973: Nixon orders the White House taping systems to be disconnected

July 23, 1973: Nixon refuses to turn over presidential tapes to the Senate Watergate Committee or the special prosecutor

oooOoooo

I don't know why the summer warranted a comrade. It was my brother Clem, and maybe it was the ruin of him.

One morning—fog lifting from the pocket of woods just beyond Yellow—I was sprawled on my stomach, watching. I knew no one else would think it beautiful. There was the plump blobby part, but also the fine branching of the new shoots that looked like the thinnest bracelets at first, then gathered into thick ropes—you never knew which way it may go.

I'd found a wrecked lounge chair with stretched plastic tethers and an old wheelless wagon in the back acre where I walked every morning and hauled them both back. In the wagon, I planted mint and marigolds.

Sometimes I left my Missing in Action bracelet in the dirt too because it had turned my wrist green. Imprinted on the nickel-colored face: PFC David D. Berkin. Had he survived? I didn't know. Many POWs had survived, and so many were still coming home. Sometimes I imagined David, only nineteen, according to the birth date on the curved bracelet I had ordered by mail, walking down the stairs of a Pan Am airplane. It would be just like we'd seen on the news: his rush into the arms of his mother, a father, maybe even a sister like me. The families all welcomed the disappeared. The disappeared tried to put on the guise of their former lives, walk down the tarmac. The disappeared carried their faces as if they would go on being welcomed. Would go on being.

What's that? Clem said, startling me from my trance.

I don't know yet, I said, as he sat down cross-legged next to me. *I'm calling it—or maybe them—Yellow.*

Them? he asked. When he wasn't around Frank, he could be okay.

Yeah, just seems like one big thing, but with a lot of parts. It's not like mushrooms cropping up next to each other—it wants to stay together. I took a stick, parting one of the branches. *Wait until tomorrow.*

Summer gathered its tomorrows slow as honey, but when I woke up the next morning, Frank sat alone watching cartoons. I passed the twins' army men hunching their guns across from each other on the picnic table. I followed a winding trail of the dull green plastic men like a disarticulated engine all the way to the pyracantha bush. When Clem saw me, he jumped up from the sagging lounge chair.

It's one thing again! he shouted.

I know. The yellow rope was intact, as if less temporary than we were.

In just-summer, Yellow had found themself.

oooo0oooo

In the eyes of Clem, Father Beck could become an astronaut. So that his lids wouldn't flutter shut during Mass, Clem imagined Father Beck taking flight, his white surplice billowing, his glasses going silver—a helmet closing over his face. Minus gravity, he would float, just like Buzz Aldrin, or like his favorite, Pete Conrad.

Father might rise like the multi-colored angels etched into the stained-glass windows. During the homily, he caught Father's droned words: *We do not fix our gaze on what is seen, but on what is unseen.* That was Corinthians. Clem could see it any way he wanted. When he squinted, one eye shut, the glow of light above the altar could be the smoke plume from the rocket, could be anything that launched the cathedral into space.

On the kneeler, Clem shifted, thinking of Pete in his space capsule, thinking of Bonny, the monkey who went to space first. Did their knees get sweaty and start to hurt like this? What did that monkey see out the window? Stars and stars and what else? Clem's mother put a bony hand on his shoulder, and he stopped fidgeting, knowing she'd send him downstairs to Catechism class with Frank.

On the kneeler, he looked up under his bangs to see Eliza was dreaming too: her dark eyes roamed the ceiling where angels fluttered, reaching their listless hands to each other. Her hands were not in prayer. She held her knotted fingers together, her knuckles white. She wore her MIA bracelet, wore it like most the girls did for one of the Army men who was still lost in a war that had already ended. They were lost, or they had vanished—he wasn't sure which. Her wrist wore a line of green from the bracelet, and now he imagined he was in the jungle with the Army men. Now, he was in the backyard. Now, he was eye level with Yellow that Eliza told him was a *they.*

A *they* fanning open, as if running along the dark wood to become something bigger, better. Eliza's eyes blinked, and her two hands came apart to hang helpless at her sides, and he wondered whether she was thinking of Yellow. Wondered if he should tell her about the bubbles that he had seen floating near Yellow. Maybe the unseen is what he saw.

What were they, those round glowing things he saw one dusk after setting his army across from the log? They rose up, hovering. Inside the bubbles, creatures with wings like moths: some scowling, some smiling.

His jaw dropped when he saw them, and they swarmed toward him, but then he looked away. When he looked back again, they were gone. Yet, they became another of the many things he knew to be true.

oooo O oooo

On one of those sultry mornings over breakfast that summer, my mother turned from the TV screen and eyed us as we took turns emptying corn flakes into our bowls. Behind her on the wavering TV screen, a man in glasses sat at a long table, testifying. A placard before him read *John Dean*. Sitting behind him, a beautiful woman with hair like ice tucked back in a bun. The face did not smile.

Y'all wanna go into the Quarter? my mother asked. Cheryl and Janice had already left for the pool, and the day stretched like a mudslide. Yellow's days were numbered, but we didn't know that yet.

I get the front seat, Frank said, pogo-hopping towards the door.

Damn it, Frank, we're not taking the car, she said. She willed her voice softer. *Let's take the streetcar in.*

Following my mother to the streetcar stop, I wondered at the way she'd coiled her hair to the base of her neck like the woman on the screen. My mother's hair was thin, a dull brown, nothing like the ice woman's. Or mine, for that matter, which was darker and thicker. Her hair kept slipping out of the bun, but she tucked it in nervously, taking my hand in hers. It was unexpected, and my heart leapt to feel the tentative dry hand in mine.

We stood waiting in the wavering sun on St. Charles Street. She wore round sunglasses. With her eyes hidden, you couldn't see her tiredness.

First, she took us to Maison Blanche where she tried on dresses. The salesgirl handed them over the top of the door, and I hung them up after they pooled to her feet.

She left the twins sitting in the chairs outside the dressing room until we heard the salesgirl yelp, then they scooted under the half door and Mama swatted their bottoms, rage-whispering between her teeth.

She didn't end up getting any of the dresses, though she looked soft and trim.

They look good, Mama, I said. *Why don't you get one?*

No money for pretty things, she said as I picked up the soft, slippery fabric—its texture like cool water. *Where would I wear them anyway?* she said.

I hadn't thought of that. On the way out of the store, she stopped at the jewelry counter and bought a pair of round earrings. She held them up, saying, *You like?*

Yes, Mama, I said. And then I did see her smile; I thought of my parents' wedding photo, how her face beamed with a kind of light I'd never seen in real life.

After we go to my reading, and—she elongated the *and—if y'all behave, we can go to Café du Monde, and I'll get you some beignets.* We didn't know what a reading was, but we didn't ask any questions, and we ended up on Bourbon Street at a place called The House of Voodoo.

Listen to Eliza, you hear, Mother said, pointing at the twins, *and if you touch anything, I'll paint your bottoms red. Anything*, she repeated.

I watched her go through a beaded doorway and sit at a small table, but then I had to keep up with the twins. The place wasn't very busy, and the cashier, a long-haired man in black with a pencil-thin mustache, stared Frank into a muted silence. Clem hovered close to me, both of us entranced by a wall of pendants, candles, and an altar with a man with the head of a goat and an effigy of a woman named Marie Laveau wearing a kerchief.

Can I go outside? Frank asked. After the third time he begged, the man said: *Hush.* I told him Frank could go outside, but only if he sat on the front stoop so I could see the back of his head the whole time.

Behind the beaded curtain, I heard my mother intone, *You don't say.* She gave her Earth Shoe a tap, as if she already knew what the person was going to say. *That's right*, the woman said back. *He's far, far away and he . . .* but then I couldn't hear anymore.

Half the room was filled with books, and the floorboards creaked as Clem and I wandered to the tall bookshelves; the books looked mysterious, filled with secrets I didn't know. Clem smiled up at me. Maybe it reminded us both of what Yellow knew and what we wanted to know.

Clem was drawn back to the goat-man and sat down cross-legged on the floor, elbows on his knees, staring into the altar.

The mustached cashier in the next room clucked his tongue and said to me, *That must be the good twin.* The shop door swung open, and the place began to fill with patrons.

I was caught in the beauty of the books' spines and the soles of my feet felt like they were riding on air. I looked around, surprised at the feeling. I thought of Yellow, the branching and magical body of them. Yellow seemed both otherworldly and yet right at home. I didn't know what they were, but this place seemed to know the truth.

The spine of a bright orange book almost glowed from the bookshelf and I was drawn toward it, though I kept my hands in the pockets of my jean shorts. *Lives of Trees: An Illustrious Book of Magic*. Again, I felt like my feet in their plain red flip flops wanted to rise from the floorboards. I looked around.

Three women stood in three corners of the room. They looked like a family—a woman with skin like black velvet and her two grown daughters, all of them with hair to their waists worn in bright red braids. They appeared like goddesses, their silence speaking to me. Even their dresses held flecks of red, and their ruby-colored braids caught the dim light, smoldering.

Why did it feel like I had wanted this moment to happen, had created it, just as Clem had created his moment? His still form sat entranced.

My body filled with a warm radiance. Like a blessing. The word itself came magically. A blessing I wanted. The women weren't looking directly at me, and yet I thought we could all feel each other's presence. Were they floating too? I opened the book to an illustration of a man sitting cross-legged, his spine radiating small disks called chakras. I remembered the photo my mother had shown me on the cover of a *Life* magazine of a monk meditating. Remembered that he did not appear to notice he was burning.

Everything clicked together like the notes to a song I once heard, long ago, maybe before I was born. The women glowed, and I felt poised for something, as if floating a few inches from the ground and Clem's small back in its striped shirt were part of the moment's fabric. In the room of thought we occupied, I felt buoyed in a word called *perfection*.

A beam of light came through the front door, hitting the row of prisms hanging between the two rooms—throwing a diffuse cloud of rainbows all around us. I smiled, feeling that the goddesses around me were smiling too. The moment rescued me.

Then the beaded door made a heavy clacking sound as my mother pulled it to one side.

Clem, she said, *what in heaven's name are you doing?*

We went to Café du Monde afterwards where Frank and Clem were back to their old ways, leaping up after eating their plate of beignets to crush paper cups under their heels.

My mother watched me so intently across the table it made me nervous. I wasn't used to being alone with her, and she took a cigarette out to smoke, tapping the tip on the table's edge.

What do you want to be when you grow up? she asked. The question jarred me, and it dropped in the silence between us. *A librarian?* I said, but my voice rose in disbelief. Never had a bookshelf like the one at the voodoo store so entranced me, yet a real library seemed boring in comparison. My mother laughed, and I was glad to see her smile.

She'd bought me the book called *The Lives of Trees*, an unexpected gift. Maybe because I held it so reverently. Maybe because the women in the room had welcomed her into that unfolding space, that room of refractory light, soft and spectral, as well.

She tapped the book in the paper bag on the table between us, protected from the fine dust of powdered sugar on the table.

Or maybe you'll be a caster of spells, she said, letting out a long cloud of cigarette smoke that drifted, then hung in the air between us.

Like Yellow, is what I thought. Yellow had arrived in our backyard to teach us something. I wished I could tell her about Yellow then, but something in my stomach caught.

I watched as her face went dreamy, staring across the street into Jackson Square with her cigarette poised between her fingertips. I found her so beautiful. But when her face turned to me, I saw that it was closing shut.

Don't tell your dad that you went to that place, you hear? she said. *Fortune-telling is a sin.* She sighed, flicking her cigarette ash into her paper cup. Clem sidled up beside me, placing his hand on the paper-cloaked book between us. My mother hastily smacked his hand.

You shall have no other gods before me. That is the first commandment. That goat creature looked like Satan, not Jesus. Don't worship Satan, Clem. I felt his body go ramrod straight next to me. His eyes flicked around, and then he retreated to Frank—the stripes on his T-shirt shimmering like a dark x-ray in the afternoon heat.

On the streetcar home, Frank jostled to be with Mama, saying it was his turn. I was glad to sit with Clem, cradling his fingers in my own. I had wanted to tell my mother about Yellow, but now understood that none of us had really changed. My mother had grown up a Catholic girl, and this day that she decided to become Mo Dean, hair in a bun, who went to The House of Voodoo to fathom the future would never happen again.

oooo O oooo

Summer nights all the fans are turned to high. The one directed into my bedroom makes me shiver in my sheets. On this night, the one of Yellow's telling, rain ticks against the window frame. Rain runs along my bloodstream. Janice and Cheryl's periods timed like their pink candy breath. I feel the pull of their blood, yet something in me resists. I never want to be so changed, never to be full woman. I begin my nightly walk through the battered, rain-slicked house, stand at the back screen door. Worry whether Yellow will melt in the ticking rain.

Moon overhead, like an eye clouded over. I put on my father's slicker—stuff my feet into Cheryl's rain boots. Screen door creaks open, my hand goes to the flaked paint on the doorframe. The backyard's a galleon surrounded by steam rising. Rain divots the grass and tree roots.

I traipse across the broken-down porch, step into the yard, and almost stumble into the twins' circle of toy army men. They look like the soldiers we see on TV, some now released from Vietnam. All I know of the war is what they show on the news, and the mysterious names of men engraved on our MIA bracelets, hoping for release, captured somewhere. And that photo on the old *Life* magazine.

This is what started it all, my mother had said. Her finger pointed at the cross-legged monk, burning. *Why did they have to print this?* Her eyes widened with sudden tears, for something I couldn't understand.

Further into the backyard, more army men rotate in small pools of rainwater. I sink into the puddles with my boot heels. Go towards the dripping moon over the plum tree. I think Yellow may be small in the rain, maybe crushed under, deflated. Instead, the steamy wet has released two bulbous forms: like one boy head and a long mollusk shape.

Yellow's fore-flank has crept over a bank of mushrooms. My bottom fits in the craftily wound roots of the black gum tree. It's as if moonlight wets my hand. I watch from beneath my father's slicker hood—his sharp boozy scent like a demented halo.

The rain slows like the ticking hand on a clock. Yellow stands still, yet I can almost feel their movement. One big thing, with all their many pulsating parts that keep growing.

Many—a word that turns over like the stars ticking overhead. I train my eye to their secret creeping. The moon's surface scuds over as the rain ceases. Long, tiered clouds reshape, cast shadows across the wet lawn. I pull my head back to feel the tree's backbone. My humanness cradles in. I doze a little. Over Yellow's glistening shape, shadows conjoin into filaments, appear to take flight.

I open my eyes wider, so I must be awake. Filaments turn to spheres, appear airborne, become a small universe of forms. They move toward me as faeries would with their uncanny lights. Closer, inside the spheres, I see their dark gray skin: winged and grinning like the fallen army men wearing their skewed helmets. One holds a miniature rifle. I duck before it fires. More come at me: wild-eyed. But only sand pellets rivet my face. Too sleepy to run, I hide under my hood. Hear the *click click click* as they empty their weapons together. Laughter rises like steam. There's the humid underground twining of tree roots, below a furred sky. It could be midnight, could be two a.m.

When the ticking stops, I peek from beneath my hood: the creatures have softened now, no longer army men at all. A honeyed slide through the air, they leave impressions like raindrops on glass. A winged light dance. Yellow's form releases beyond them—its muscles give way and mine do too. The faeries wear only their illuminated skin. The tender inside of me wants to feel the tender inside of them. Where there were many voices, now there is only one.

One side loves the other. The thought inside my head could be theirs, could be Yellow's. The faeries with their soft honey forms turn bright as bees, whirr as branches drip. I lick my lips, find my left nipple: its flat possibility. Feel it rise sensorial as these forms.

One side loves the other. The thought again. From me? From Yellow? I don't know, but I know that the faerie forms darken first, firing pellets, reenact their little murders, then change back into glistening forms of light. My eyes fill, and my fingers find both nipples. My chest once like armor has released, too; maybe I'm just beginning to become woman. *Become multiplicity*, Yellow's thought says. I don't know what that means. But I do know, without having the language for it, that Yellow's breathing billows the steam of this temporary world.

Trees do too, Yellow says. I look up into the black gum's spatulate, leafy hands waving their own language. I can only gasp, and the faeries sigh in time with the thrushing of tree hands. Who will know, in time, but Yellow and me, that I cry. Not just for the joy, but for the pain too. For everything.

oooo0oooo

The next morning, I slept in, too late to protect Yellow from Frank. The twins sat at the picnic table outside with their cereal bowls. The rest of the household still asleep as fog burned off the trees like smoke.

I know what you've been looking at back there, Frank said. *It's like insect guts!*

Or a mushroom pillow! Clem said.

It's like upchuck, Frank said.

Dog upchuck, Clem said, his face eagerly reflecting Frank's.

Clem and me wanna throw it back and forth like Jello, right? Clem nodded.

Or, he ventured, *maybe we can leap on it like a trampoline!* Frank nodded.

Or shoot it with our Nerf guns, Clem said.

Why are you going along with him, Clem? I told you to leave it alone.

You showed me what Yellow can do, Eliza. I just wanted Frank to see it.

You infiltrated! I said. Not even sure where I got the word. *Why did you infiltrate?*

I marched to the rear of the yard and found Yellow as I'd left them the night before. Bigger, even grander from the rain. The puffed body lounged across the steamy log. The faeries now seemed part of a marvelous dream; maybe one I'd never have again.

Frank and Clem had trailed behind me; when I faced them, Frank smeared a trail of grime across his mouth.

If you do anything to Yellow, I told them, *they will know and remember.*

They? Frank asked.

They—because they just want to be one thing, Clem said, his shoulders dropping.

You're weird, Frank retracted his body.

Clem's right . . . I shrugged. *They're not a he, not a she.*

I made them swear they would not touch them or talk about them. Their blue eyes went solemn under their thatches of wheat-colored hair. How could

I tell them apart? In Frank's, the sure and solid belief in his own liberty and his own desires. In Clem's, something easily shakable.

He did whatever Frank wanted. Until he didn't.

I'm telling Mom, Frank said.

I didn't know what to do, so I told one of the first lies I would tell. To protect Yellow, I said to myself. Not to hurt Clem.

That afternoon, hands on my hips, my voice shaking with anger, I told them if they ever told Mom, something might happen to her. I didn't know what, but it wouldn't be good. It was Clem's blue eyes that widened with fear. I felt a pang in my heart when I said it, but the moment had already passed for regret.

oooo0oooo

Secrets occlude, have occlusion. Like the transom window in our time-worn house.

Something overheard—the frosted window ajar. How does one lock the other out? My mother's back to me a kind of occlusion. My father's blunt face, soured by drink, never a secret. At school, my friend Mollie used to label her notes SECRET, and by that she also meant *open me, open me, open*. Mother's secret trip to The House of Voodoo was safe; now the twins had theirs: Yellow.

After it happened, only to Yellow would I tell what I knew—my secret. It was also the day I split Yellow open: the bodiless body, the mindless mind, then watched them re-gender, regenerate, find themself, then heal themself.

Stitching mind to mind, heedless of my anger, heedless of my shame, and what made me tear them in two.

ooooOoooo

Before Yellow, Clem knew nothing about the general principles of gravity.

He was just a boy, after all.

Before Yellow, he would dream his sister wandering their two-story house at night.

Maybe when he dreamed her, she was pacing between the tall window shadows, stepping lightly through the window's heart, the large black gum outside rustling its leaves and tossing in a late wind.

Storms as they moved through like a premonition of rain, of drowning.

Before Yellow, he wasn't just a twin, he was an extension, an expansion of Frank.

Where Frank's eyes went, Clem made his vision subject. They saw together, when they saw.

But after Yellow, after Yellow's stretching, their slow engulfing thought, Clem began to know that the dream of his sister walking sleepless through the house was a dream too, was the dreaming behind a million eyes.

After Yellow, Clem began to dream of being weightless, spinning to the ends of a universe he was just beginning to know.

After Yellow, Clem looked up into the sky, hoping to see the astronauts, thinking of them floating inside their space capsule.

What's up is whatever is over your head, what's below—the ungrounded ground.

In space, Clem knew, there was nothing to push against—a body without leverage, without any resistance at all.

Like floating with Frank in their first watery home—the mother ship.

These thoughts, when he said them aloud, began to fracture Frank away from Clem.

In their shadowy room, where Clem would tell him these thoughts, where the window was open and a million insects ticked, hummed, and hit the screen, the words landed hard, and Frank said nothing back.

Frank began to look through him, rather than with him.

Clem stopped saying *Yellow* to Frank, told him instead about Skylab and all the discoveries there.

Every discovery that Yellow transported into the small universe of Clem's bigger mind.

oooOoooo

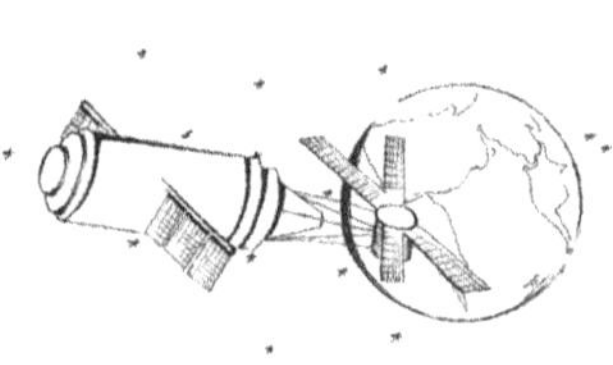

Skylab Timeline

May 14, 1973: Skylab launched in space. Seconds into launch, encounters undetectable damage to solar panels

May 25, 1973: Skylab 2's crew of three—Captain Pete Conrad, Joe Kerwin, and Paul Weitz launched to man space station and to repair damage to Skylab

oooOoooo

I think it's a natural question: why explore space? . . . To my way of thinking, part of human nature is to reach out and explore.

Paul Weitz, Skylab 2 crew

Interspace exploration provides this spiritual quality. It allows you to go to the unknown and find what's there and hopefully you're going to improve your lot.

Alan Bean, Skylab 3 crew

Skylab represents a definite turning point. After three record-breaking missions, we have new theories about the universe.

Pete Conrad, Commander, Skylab 2

oooоOoooo

Interviewer: *So the purpose of Skylab was primarily to discover the effect of long-duration spaceflight on the human body?*

Astronaut K: *You could say that. But there were other benefits. Three different crews orbited Skylab for a total of six years; we conducted over 270 experiments. I should say that our commander, Pete Conrad, made sure we had fun while we were at it.*

Interviewer: *But from the get-go, Skylab started with complications. Is that correct?*

Astronaut K: *Sixty-three seconds into launch a micrometeoroid shield opened. Designed to protect Skylab from debris and function as a thermal blanket, the shield tore off.*

When our crew met up with Skylab ten days later, we had the task of repairing the solar shield. The Marshall Center in Huntsville, Alabama came up with three solutions; we tested them underwater like we usually did, but we weren't weightless. We weren't in space.

It wasn't simple, and then it was.

Interviewer: *What preparations were made for Skylab's launch?*

Astronaut K: *There's a story I've never forgotten. Before NASA sent up Skylab—this would be the late '60s—they wanted to test the effects of long-duration spaceflight. So NASA launched a monkeyed satellite. Always better, the thinking went, to send up a monkey before men. Biosatellite 3 housed the monkey. His name was Bonny, a macaque, affectionately called the Astromonk, selected from a group of about a half dozen raised for this purpose. They chose the most alert and the most physically sound. The one they figured could withstand the duration of the mission: thirty days rotating Earth, just like the Skylab astronauts would do.*

Day Five, the monkey quit participating in the game to receive food pellets. Day Six, he quit drinking water. His heart rate sunk to sixty, and it was decided to deorbit Bonny on Day Eight. He died hours after splashdown. What the scientists didn't think through were the constraints on Bonny. He was restrained in the cold spacecraft and could only move his hands and feet. He was given an inadequate amount of food and water, and he urinated more than usual, as happens in space.

And let's remember, he was alone. I know from being up there that your muscles get starved for oxygen. While the Astromonk was out there, rotating the planet, staring at God knows what—did they even give him a window?

I don't even know, but maybe not entirely coincidentally, two of the monkeys he was raised with died on Earth. Two of his friends, maybe his brothers, died while his heartbeat was slowing. What do you make of that?

[Silence]

Interviewer: *How many days were you in orbit?*

Astronaut K: *Twenty-eight.*

oooo0oooo

It's not my body that clicked into place when I first saw Yellow. No. You could call it mind, or you could call it heart, or you could call it a translucence. That sentience conjoining us so that everything in me was that god, that universe.

oooоOoooo

Interviewer: *Sounds like it wasn't a cakewalk to start.*

Astronaut K: *We were still a troubled mission until June 7 when we got ready to go out the door to repair the solar panels.*

Before we left Earth, Rusty had led the crew in the Marshall water tank, so we could devise an extravehicular activity—what we call an EVA—to go out the side and make the repair. There were no handholds, no footholds, no visual aids, no lights on the outside of the spacecraft because there was no planned maintenance—too dangerous. The only planned EVA for the mission was to retrieve and exchange film in the Apollo Telescope Mount at the top of the craft.

Interviewer: *Ah, yes, the ATM.*

Astronaut K: *Right. For this unexpected repair to the shield, all we had were the suits and umbilicals that tethered us to the craft, and we brought up the tools that we thought we'd need. They had planned an EVA that had us erect a twenty-five-foot pole, put the cable cutter on the end of it, and the jaws—which were about three inches long—had to close around the aluminum strap and bite halfway into it, but not all the way. Now we'd have a handhold, and Conrad could go along the handrail while I stabilized the near end of it. He had another rope attached to his sleeve and once he got as far out as he could, taking care not to touch any sharp edges, he would hook that rope down into the solar panel cover as far down as possible to give it some leverage from the hinge. What we had to do was not only cut the strap, but then break up that hinge which had frozen and start that thing up.*

He was to go down to the panel, put the rope on, and then I would tie the other end of the rope to a stanchion as close to the surface as possible, and then the two of us would get under the rope, stand up, and hope for the best. That was the Rusty Schweikert solution. We went out with all our equipment; I even had a dental saw from the medical kit taped to the chest of my suit, and I thought, well, if all else fails, I might have to go down and cut that thing.

We did have a couple extra tethers—six-foot equipment tethers with hooks on both ends. This proved to be crucial to the mission. When we went out there, getting around to the area was no problem, erecting the twenty-five-foot pole with the ropes was no problem, but we were a good twenty feet away and couldn't get any closer to the aluminum strap. Getting the jaws onto the strap close enough with no foot restraints was proving to be impossible.

Interviewer: *What was your job?*

Astronaut K: *I had the pole in my hand and would move it toward the jaws trying to gauge whether I was exactly far enough, and when I did that, my body would start turning, Newton's third law, and Conrad was trying to grab my legs with one arm and a strut with another arm, but that wasn't a stable enough platform and we went nuts for one dayside pass and failed. Just didn't do it.*

Here comes nightside and we're sitting inside the cabin thinking about it, and we saw outside on Skylab's fuselage an eyebolt. It was a circular bolt, looks like the end of a Yale lock on the surface of the workshop near one of the antennas. Right in line! It appeared from nowhere; it didn't appear at all while we trained. No accounting for it! Don't know what it's there for, but we're thinking, what if I'm strapped to the eyebolt?

Interviewer: *Sounds like a miracle . . .* [clearing his throat]

Astronaut K: *Without a doubt! So we got that extra tether, and there's a hook on the front of my suit, flipped it through the eyebolt, and tightened it up. Now I have a three-point suspension to stand up and place my feet on the surface of the workshop, and suddenly I'm as stable as a rock, can almost straighten my knees all the way out. It's like standing in your garden at home. Man, it was wonderful. Two minutes later the job was done.*

The rest of it unfolded as I said: we crawled under the rope that Pete had laid out. Probably the most dangerous part of the space walk was Pete going down there amid all that debris, but he got away with it, and we stood up.

Suddenly, it released on us, and we both went ass over teakettle into outer space! Luckily, our EVA system was an umbilical—a nice stout one with an eight-inch steel cable in the middle of it—so we didn't have any worries about that. We went out to the end of those long umbilicals and then hand-over-handed ourselves back to something we could hang on to.

We turned around and the prettiest sight I've ever seen in my life was that solar panel cover fully deployed at 90 degrees. You could see the panels starting to come out as they warmed up in the sun, and we knew we had done the job.

So that was great. It was a rather short EVA. We went down to the sun-end of the ATM, to sort of get a pre-look at the film retrieval route.

Interviewer: *So you also had a second part to the mission, right?*

Astronaut K: *A quick one: you go up to the sunny end of the ATM, it's the middle of the day now, and this thing is pointed at the sun and the Earth is below you, and you can stand up in foot restraints there and you are king of the hill.* [Laughing. Full grin.]

Here you are standing up, and the Earth is spread out horizon to horizon. There is nothing like looking at the world through the helmet of a space suit; it's much better than a hatch. You just feel like you are in the middle of this big Cinerama movie! That was a heck of an experience! It was over in less than three hours, but that was the best day of the flight.

Interviewer: *Quite a remarkable three hours.*

Astronaut K: *Mmmmm . . .* [Nodding, smiling.]

oooоOoooo

Late May, my sister took us to Lake Pontchartrain. Cheryl just got her license and at first, she was magnanimous, saying we would have the best day without our parents. The twins jumped off the sofa into the pool of the blue shag carpet. Glee-filled, almost dotty. My mother yelled: *Stop it, Clem. Stop it, Frank.*

They'd been named after dead grandfathers and hated their old-timey names. Just as I had been named after my mother's favorite old aunt. In the photo my mother once showed me, my great-aunt had a giant nose and wore delicate gold-rimmed spectacles. *A math teacher*, my mother told me. *Like an eagle with those eyes*, she said. *She took me in when your bitch grandmother threw me out.*

I touched the photo, and my mother slapped my hand when a brownish edge fell away.

We left our battered house that day in our parents' '69 finned Chevy, Cheryl and Janice laughing in the front seat. The three of us lined up in the back—me in the middle to keep Frank from knocking Clem on the head.

Cheryl drove to where the smooth, dark stairs around the lake made a curve. There was a small point out onto the water, with one low tree.

oooo0oooo

Lake water looking soured and cloudy, kicked over. My toes clench at dense, silty sand. Frank and Clem throw clods at each other out on the rocky point. Teenage boys have found my sisters, flat out on their stomachs on beach towels, straps down. My sisters' voices manufactured for just this purpose. Rising, falling, laughing—but too hard.

A man has left a group gathered around a portable charcoal grill at the top of the lake stairs. He wears aviator frames, commas framing his mouth. His cheeks divoted with small scars. My palms cup the water around my body. I sink to the soft lakebed with eyes open. The man's body is fishy-white moving towards me. He drags each leg against some force I cannot see. Beneath water, I wonder about Yellow: could they swim? Float? When I rise to the surface, my lips pop open for air.

The man, less than four feet away now, holds a silver cylinder of beer—JAX—the can gleams back. He turns slightly away, looking out across to the other side of the lake, a palm shading his eyes, despite the sunglasses.

What's your name? he says. I tell him, and he's never heard of a girl named that. *I'll call you Lizzy.* The man's breasts are slightly droopy. Gray hair has sprung up on his chest. I start to swim away, but he catches my foot.

Hey, I say. He laughs, and just like that, drags me toward him. *Stop*, I say. But for some reason I'm laughing too. *Stop,* I repeat. The side of my head and ear slide along the water's surface.

Oh, he says flatly, letting go. There's laughter on the shore—strangers meeting and talking.

Why not me?

You're okay, he smiles. *Aren't you?*

Yes, I say, bobbing upright.

Lizzy, are you a lezzy?

What's a lezzy? I ask.

Lesbian. I blink slowly. When I do, he grabs my hand and pulls it toward him. And then my hand is on his crotch. Something rises under my hand. *You like this, don't you?* I pull it away, start to swim back to shore, but I'm slow. I've always been slow in water. *Lezzy*, he says in a mock high voice. *Don't leave me.*

And I don't scream. In fact, my face is trapped in the echo of his smile, as if spellbound.

You liked that, right?

No, I mouth, and he reaches toward me again. There are voices on shore, but they don't call me back; they don't even see us. Like we're trapped in a time without sensation or alarm.

Maybe you're not a lesbian after all. He crouches with his beer, and I'm still frozen.

His hand snakes into my swim bottoms, jams two fingers in me. My chest clenches—I may have stopped breathing.

There's a secret I have to tell you, I say to Yellow later. *I have to tell you.* Tears come fast and hard, and I hate the salt strafing my face. I'm on my side in the prickly grass, some of it just dirt. My vagina is aflame. His rough fingers have left a trail of blood in my swim pants.

Only in the car afterward do I know that I'm the one bleeding, packed between my brothers in the backseat. I'm still frozen, have become an absence. They spit on each other; some of it falls on my legs. When the man reached for me again, I did nothing.

I don't have to tell Yellow that. Because they know it. My sobbing tells them everything. But their silence angers me. The rotten plums have gone past blued skins to purple to black. A heap of chattering mouths. Sobs wrack my body, and I take the few hard fruits left and throw them into Yellow. Standing above what looks like dog vomit.

Dog vomit, I say to Yellow. *You're dog vomit.* I pound Yellow with plums over and over. She absorbs one; he absorbs one. They wrinkle around the plums to accept them. My gut wants to retch watching it. My body has been shivering all along.

oooo〇oooo

I huddled next to Yellow like a warm animal two mornings after our trip to the lake, afraid that the tail-end of my morning's dream may come true. Why had the dream fallen over me like a troubled shadow?

In my dream, I was older than I could ever imagine. I wore glasses, my hair cut short and graying. I looked through the dark window, washing dishes, when a fear overtook me.

Would I want my husband to work during the day when I was alone or at night when I would be alone, or would the fear always occupy my thoughts?

In the dream, I didn't know who spoke. But the voice said, *You are that fear. You are that dark through the window.*

When I woke, I wondered first at the idea of being so old, then the suffused fear of being so trapped in that house, in that terrible drama. In that future, men protected you from other men who stared at women in the dark.

I huddled next to Yellow, took a breath, then blew onto Yellow's surface.

You are that fear, Yellow said. I startled up, staring at the still-quivering surface.

The words weren't said aloud. They formed like clouds in my mind.

When I went inside the house, the Watergate hearings droned on. Men's voices questioned other men. My mother stood at the window, doing dishes, looking out at the empty street.

I thought of the monk who had made her so angry, his face so peaceful while flames licked across his body. He was not fear.

At the sink, my mother's limbs moved rigidly, as if her very bones were about to shatter.

oooo O oooo

After Skylab, we have new theories about the universe—so Commander Pete Conrad said. But we already did. We just didn't know what those theories were exactly.

At Princeton, Pete looked out his dorm room window and watched a disheveled man with wild, white hair carrying a book stuffed with bookmarks, talking to himself. Pete was concerned, but his roommate reassured him.

That, he said, *is Albert Einstein, and in that book are all the paychecks he has neglected to cash. He's got an IQ of five hundred, and he's the father of quantum physics! But he doesn't understand money.*

Or it just doesn't matter to him, Pete said back.

Stories circulate, stories animate the human, take flight, veer in every direction. Stories are how we know about a person, even if it's actually all about the narrator of the story being told.

What mattered to Pete when he busted his ass to get to Princeton on a Navy scholarship was flying. When he was flunking out of Haverford Prep because he couldn't read right, that desire to fly impelled him to ride his Indian motorbike shirtless with a Lucky cigarette clutched between his teeth across campus. He held the record for most demerit hours earned in under twenty seconds.

He learned to fly a Piper from a woman who had trained WASPs in WWII. She captured his sixteen-year-old heart. After his first solo flight back and forth to Scranton, he planted a kiss on her cheek and then, when she backed away shaking her head—understood. But he loved her anyway or maybe because she only loved women, and he kept flying weekends. He became an aviator in the Navy and called his mother when he landed for the first time on an aircraft carrier.

After he married and had three boys of his own, he responded to the invite to 110 US citizen candidates to *become our twentieth-century Mercury, orbiting Earth in space!* The newly minted NASA did their best to mind-scramble the mostly active-duty military test pilot applicants with endurance tests galore.

Who's the god among you? That's what NASA wanted them to compete for—god status. Pete lasted eleven days and left his enema bag on the commander's desk on his exit.

But there was something about Pete: the small, balding trickster who made everyone laugh. Before Skylab, on Apollo 12, Pete was the third man to walk on the moon. Before Apollo, there was Gemini 11, and before that, Gemini 5, when he and Gordon Cooper were stuffed in a spacecraft with their knee muscles going dry. In *chimp mode* for sure.

Eight days in a garbage can is what Pete called it. He and Gordo ran out of stories. System failures meant they could only drift in orbit and sit, listening to Al Hirt records beamed up to them from Mission Control while their trash floated around their metal helmets. For eight hours every day, Mission Control went silent, and because his body ached, he couldn't sleep. Occasionally, *Gemini* would vent hydrogen and oxygen which forced the spacecraft to rotate away from the one glorious thing they could see out their window: the marbled landforms of Earth. He stared into darkness and the deepest silence you'll ever know. *It was the loneliest I have ever been on a flight*, he said.

Though Einstein called it *spooky action at a distance*, quantum entanglement enables two particles to affect each other across time and space. Maybe that explains the Astromonk languishing in his capsule and his brothers who died in sympathy on Earth. Maybe quantum entanglement explains why, when a body rotates away from that which once beheld it, we know darkness, and we know suffering.

oooo0oooo

The White House taping system was turned off July 18, 1973, only days after it became public knowledge during the televised hearings.

Some people forget that Nixon's refusal to release the White House tapes upon subpoena was the reason for his impeachment.

So many people put their imaginings into an absence: in this case, the erasure of eighteen minutes of a meeting between his chief of staff and Nixon that occurred on June 20, 1972, just three days after the Watergate break-in.

At issue: our imaginings about what silence holds. A deafening silence.

Rose Mary Woods, his secretary, claimed to have accidentally erased just five minutes of the tape. At the end of five minutes, one tone is replaced by a deeper one.

Alexander Haig, in an interview, said, *Perhaps there had been one tone applied by Miss Woods . . . and then perhaps some sinister force had come in and applied the other energy source and taken care of the information on that tape.*

Judge Sirica broke in and asked Haig: *Has anyone ever suggested who that sinister force might be?*

Haig said, *No, your Honor.*

Later, much later, most believe that Haig himself erased the rest of the tape. Rose Mary's accidental erasure was maybe five minutes. Perhaps not coincidentally, sources say Haig and Nixon circled the White House in the back of the presidential limo one afternoon. Was there fumbling? One man pushing the recorder to the other?

Many speculate that during that drive, the sinister force was Haig himself, responsible for the deeper tone and the deletion needed.

In the cosmology of the self, the demon serves as our attachments personified. Did Haig know the sinister force as himself—the dark spark of the human that wants and wants?

oooo0oooo

Thich Quang Duc was the Buddhist monk in the photo that her mother showed Z on the cover of *Time* magazine. An image Z could never dispel. June 11, 1963.

The beauty of his profile, so still even as the flames wrinkle and waver around him.

If only, were words Z's mother often said, when she said anything at all.

Duc was protesting the death of nine Buddhists—including two children crushed under armored personnel carriers at the behest of Vietnam's President Diem, a Catholic.

The army killed them for celebrating the birthday of Gautama Buddha on May 8, 1963. *Phat Dan*, they called it. Duc had been a hermit for three years in the mountains of Vietnam when he led 350 monks and nuns to the Cambodian Embassy, then sat quietly as five gallons of petrol were poured on his head.

Once the match was lit, people screamed, but Duc's fellow monks lay down and blocked the firefighters from saving him.

Thich Quang Duc *never moved a muscle, never uttered a sound*, a reporter wrote. The man was no longer a body, but a consciousness made manifest. The conflagration of some wild heart.

Z's mother hated that photo that had been plastered across every front-page newspaper in America. They say it drew the Americans into that helpless, hopeless war.

The picture that changed the world, Time captioned it.

That's exactly what her mother's lover told her.

He left for Vietnam when Z was eight.

Z's eyes were dark like her father's, not the vivid blue of her mother's other children. Her mother named her Eliza without even asking her husband.

If anyone thought to look in the attic, in the humid flesh-colored boxes breaking apart, they could have found the letters tied with cracking rubber bands. There were less than a dozen.

Z's father had last written to her mother just a few days before he was caught in friendly fire. The letters had been sent to her mother's post office box that no one, least of all her husband, knew that she had secured.

Of course, no one would ever know what the date March 8, 1972 meant to her. Her mother only learned about it through St. Catherine's phone tree when he died. The abrupt call from Marie one street over. Z's mother gasped, and Marie said, *I know! Poor Lou-Ann and the kids.* Her mother knew every year when she stood near his grave on Memorial Day. If his family was there, she knew to come back after they'd gone.

After the accident, Z's sister Cheryl told her that her mother was on her way to DC. *Remember how she had that obsession about going to the graveyard on Memorial Day?*

Not really, Z said.

Well, she really wanted to see the Vietnam Memorial in DC. That's where she was headed. But like everything else she wanted to do, Dad wouldn't let her go.

But she did go, Z said.

Yeah, but she didn't make it.

oooo0oooo

You remember Mr. Greco from St. Catherine, don't you? my mother asked, but I didn't. My mother had left the babies home napping with Cheryl and Janice and taken me to the French Quarter. *Let's go shop while we have time*, she said.

The man looking at me was the greengrocer. Mama said she always went on Tuesdays when we were in school, and they had the best vegetables. I didn't know what that meant until we got to the A&P, and the man in a white coat with his name curlicued on his front pocket looked down at me. He was piling tomatoes into pyramids, plucking out the ones that were too soft and putting them in a box.

I must have been around eight then. I wanted to hide behind my mother, but I was too old for that. The man wore black-framed glasses and had a crew-cut. I wondered what his spiky black hair would feel like under the palm.

My mother seemed happier than when we'd arrived, just moments before. In the car, she'd snapped at me to comb my hair and to quit twisting my bracelet. She talked in a high, nervous voice, and she'd stared into the rear-view, covering her glossy nose with powder from her compact mirror.

The man has a fuzzy quality to me now, his features indistinct. My mother asked me whether I knew Jenny and Stephen from church, but I didn't know them either. *His family lives in another parish, but they go to St. Catherine for Mass.*

The man stood stiffly—it was like there were walls of ice between us. And though I did not fiddle with my bracelet once, my mother twisted her hands together like birds she had to tame.

Behind him, because it was summer, there was a carefully balanced pile of watermelon, and someone shoved their cart too fast and hard, so one dark green fruit at the top wobbled like a planet. I pointed a finger, but by the time Mr. Greco turned, it had rolled down the pyramid and hit the Formica floor. The watermelon's red insides were vivid and jagged—the seeds like eyes that did not blink shut. He and my mother backed away from each other, and Mr. Greco nodded curtly.

It really was his job to clean it up, my mother said once we were back in the hot car. *There was nothing else to say anyway.* She was talking to herself, I realized. And I watched from the backseat as her jaw trembled, and as she wiped the tears from her face.

I never understood why we'd gone. My mother hadn't bought any vegetables.

Do we still need to go shopping, Mama? I asked.

For heaven's sake, Eliza. Of course we do. Let's stop at the Piggly Wiggly. She braked hard when we pulled up.

Those eyes, those eyes, she said, shaking her head and looking at me in the rear view. He'd taken off his glasses once, rubbing the lenses on his white coat. One dark eye strayed just a little to the side. I didn't know what she meant, but I never saw him again.

PART II

oOo

The forgetting had its own dimensions: the past and what she thought she knew about Yellow.

Barely seen, as in the shadow at the corner of Jackson Square, the one that flitted away the closer you came to it.

The forgetting could be buoyant, and it could be sticky.

Because Z had become identity, had lost the shadowy edges of herself. She was a she now, third person—an observer. She had crushes on girls and on boys. And in that case, was she really a she? She didn't know.

By seventeen, her senior year, she'd grown to her full height of 5'3"; her dark hair was cut short, eyes snarled with eyeliner.

She and Glen had the alliance of two or three other misfits hanging out near the darkroom after Yearbook. Though most of the time, it was just the two of them.

Janice got married to her high school sweetheart and lived near Shreveport while her husband served in the Army. She would have her third baby in November. Janice did not name one of the yowling babies after their parents.

Cheryl had stayed in Atlanta after graduating from Georgia State. The rare times he showed up for Mass, her father would always talk to Father Beck about his daughter, *the accountant*.

Our one success story, Mama would join in. On top of the TV console in the living room, Mama fanned out the postcards Cheryl sent every week that she traveled out of state.

In the sticky heat of her bedroom, sometimes Z stood naked in front of the antique mirror that once belonged to that old great-aunt Eliza she was named after. Her small breasts were still of little consequence, as was the dark thatch of her pubis.

What fascinated her most were the blue veins she could follow under her pale skin.

Like vines, they branched away from her sternum to form filigrees of blue as they traveled to each areola. One vein almost purplish where it ended at her left breast.

The blue blood coursed through her like everyone's blue blood that could become at a moment, or in a moment, only a remembrance. She could almost feel what love felt like as her veins flowered from her heart just as trees undulated from their roots and expanded their fierce languages of desire.

Just as her blood coursed, Yellow had coursed along the rotting log, had overtaken the log, becoming more than, not less than.

And then from the kitchen, a glass broke where her mother stood at the kitchen sink, and Z forgot again.

oOo

High school, like everything else, is never what you think it will be. In 1979, the standard-issue cliques found their spaces: band geeks wearing their orbital mouth gear playing the snare drums outside the auditorium, the jocks slouching outside the gym wearing their Saints jerseys or maybe a T-shirt advertising that they'd gone down to Bourbon Street to drool over the strippers. On Fridays, when they didn't have to wear their uniforms, you'd see Buford or Beau wearing one of those T-shirts to first period, and then the principal would pull them out of class, give them a whipping, and they'd be wearing their high school jerseys again, still puffing their chests out with pride.

Z's only outlet was Yearbook where the *artsy-fartsy kids*, so named by the cheerleaders, hung out in Mr. Pageant's room, even during lunch period, when he walked home to his two standard poodles. They designed two-page spreads highlighting the popular kids as instructed, but in subtle ways they undermined the very concept of popularity and showed them for the craven ego-hounds they were. Like Z's big idea to take the Homecoming Court pictures at the above-ground tombs in St. Louis Cemetery. The high school cast of characters sauntered in wearing their satiny dresses and peach tuxes and the Yearbook staff perched them on the tops of graves when the tour guides weren't looking. Z acted like a serious assistant as they set up every shot, never forgetting the details: like the garbage bags that she smoothed under Mandy DeBoyce's fuchsia number and fly swatters that she handed to The Royal Couple and took away before the shutter clapped down. Jill Jeffries' hideous makeup ran because they made her sit so long on the stoop next to Marie Leveau's triple x-marked grave.

Why are you putting me here? Jill crowed. *It's dirty.*

You're dirty, Glen whispered between his teeth as he clicked his Minolta.

You two encourage each other, Mr. Pageant often said. Especially when Glen told Z to line each page of the Homecoming Court photos with the lyrics from that season's Top Ten song, "Dust in the Wind." Imagine Jill's rabbity overbite next to the half-blackened tomb spiraled with the lines from the song about our eventual dissolution into dust.

Mr. Pageant approved every page with the flourish of his signature because he found their humor as funny as Glen and Z did.

oOo

Forgetting made her solid, real to herself and full of grudges that she carried in her Army Surplus backpack: her mother's twisted mouth, her father's glassy eyes, her sisters' assessing words, Clem's nonsense that danced in his eyes.

These were the things she told Glen about when they took the bus to the French Quarter and walked around Jackson Square, looking at the artists with their easels, the tarot readers throwing down infinite fortunes to the tourists, who all gaped at the what and the who of Crescent City.

Other times, she forgot who to love and why. She and Glen got shit-faced on a bottle of Boone's Farm and crawled into a parked carriage, laughing as the old horse whinnied and shook the reins. What was in Z that she took Glen's hands and put them on her breasts? Glen barked, *Girl, you need some padding,* pulling his hands away. She wanted to crawl out of the edges of herself. She forgot she wasn't equipped for love.

The next day, despite their hangovers, Glen looked her dead in the eye over the lunch table and said: *You know I'm not built for women, and you're not built for men, right?*

But she didn't. She did not know either of those things. Or she'd forgotten.

oOo

Z was trying to forget, but Clem could not.

The twins were fourteen by then, and Frank had developed solid muscles, playing JV football, while Clem stayed thin and rangy, growing his hair longer than anyone else's in ninth grade. Much to his father's disgust.

Clem didn't understand why Z kept retreating from what they had both understood years ago.

They're more than we are, Z had told him, one of those dusky evenings in 1973. *But I'm starting to think they are us.* She looked puzzled, *because I saw those beings in the air, because I hear them thinking, because . . .* and then her eyes had clouded. When she smiled, huddled under the thin limbs of the plum tree, and when he watched Yellow's branched and luminous body, Clem felt something like a door opening.

That evening, not so many years ago, Yellow's faint quivers were the same as the prickling wind on his own skin. In just one moment, everything he touched could fall away, and Clem knew Z felt it too. They must have been there for hours because they seemed to float on their backs until the stars moved in and the planets shifted over them, but to Clem it was just one weightless entry into space.

He tried to bring her back—to pull her from some cliff she couldn't even see in front of her. But Clem began to understand that the cliff where she stood was the one before college. In less than a month, Z would be leaving home and going to New York City. She was looking beyond Clem, beyond it all. But he still had to try.

Just the other day, Clem had said to Z: *Yellow is the hand of god.*

Z squinted her eyes to look at him closely and said, *You're beginning to worry me.*

Lately, he'd been so concerned about Skylab's reentry that even their father noticed.

When's your rocket ship landing, Clem? their dad asked, hunkered behind a sticky row of ribs that he pulled apart with cigar-stained teeth then flung down on a plastic plate. Their mother usually just hovered for dinner, never really sitting down but bringing things back and forth from the kitchen with a cigarette clutched in her mouth. Clem duly reported the situation of Skylab.

Any day now, Dad. NASA's performing a maneuver so that Skylab won't hit land. They want it to disintegrate into the Atlantic Ocean. His eyes flitted around the backyard, resting on the trees in the corner where Yellow once thrived. Z wasn't looking that way, even though they both knew the secret of Yellow's escape. *They've timed it—the maneuver—it should take about eighteen minutes, which is what they need . . .*

Clem didn't have time to finish before his father's hand came towards his chin, looking ready to cuff him, but slow enough that Clem had time to pull his head back.

What the hell, Clem, do you really think I give a crap? his father laughed. Clem turned to Z next to him, searching her eyeliner-thickened eyes.

Maybe because she was already half-gone from their battered house, Z merely raised one plucked eyebrow and rested a small hand on his shoulder for a moment. Frank laughed with his father, in his standard wiseacre guffaw. That was the worst of it: for Clem to see the mirror of his own face twisted in derision at himself.

Just the opposite of love, his heart spoke.

Z sat up straight, her face slightly gray.

I don't like eating the flesh of . . . She let the ribs drop to her plate. *What is this? Pig? Do you like it, Clem?*

Clem shrugged, his shoulders collapsed, his eyes widened.

Their mother swooped in on a raven's wing.

What's your bellyaching about, Eliza? she said.

I don't want to eat meat anymore, Mama. It makes me . . . Z stood up, trying to disentangle her legs from the picnic table where they sat. And then she vomited on the oilcloth that their father had bolted to the top of the table he'd made.

Clem watched the sickness of the family mount in waves around him.

oOo

The fall of 1981, Z was set loose in NYC, going to Barnard on a scholarship for studio art and art history. She no longer had her boy body but already knew—and didn't care—that her small breasts and plain sharp face weren't attractive to most men.

She did not know who she was, Z decided in college.

In Life Drawing, freshman year, she was aroused by a model's large nipples and then the next week, by a man's small compact scrotum. Who or what was she to desire both?

She'd accepted the scholarship to college, spurred on to apply by her high school guidance counselor and by her art teacher, who believed in her, or so they said. Her parents thought it madness to study art, but she was the third girl to *grow out,* as her mother called it, and they wanted her to be a Cheryl rather than a Janice, so they gave her exactly $1000 a year, as long as she kept a job and asked for no more. They made it clear she would be on her own after graduation.

And don't bother to come crying home, her father wrote in a terse note with the check. The money barely paid for anything, but she felt lucky and free and didn't mind washing her underwear and sweaters in the dorm bathroom sink for the week.

Every sacrifice was worth it. New York City clattered with souvlaki carts, honking taxis, strange-eyed passersby, and inspiration. She spent weekends as a student resident exploring the heaven of the Met for free. Over a million works of art in the permanent collection, with seventeen curated departments. She vowed in her first year that she would explore every wing in the four years she had at college, to look deeply and long into the art that moved her. She held to her self-imposed project for the first two months, spending one day out of her weekend prowling the echoing halls for new sources of inspiration and obsession.

She left the sour-smelling dorm room in the residential hall that she shared with Dot Sandusky and took the subway, loading her backpack with her weekend reading, her sketchbook, and her best charcoal pencils. She and Dot had little in common, yet they clung to each other for their first year.

Face it, Dot told her. *We are out-of-towners and extreme wallflowers. We only have each other.*

Dot was going to major in physics and spent weekend mornings studying in her bed, her wild hair massed around her pale face, pawing at her fingerprint-spotted glasses, drawing intricate graphs in black ink in a spiral notebook, and telling Z to walk more quietly. Dot had arrived from Kansas City and used the line from the *Wizard of Oz* too much for Z's liking. Her boyfriend had stayed home, driving from his parents' house to KSU to save money for their wedding. She wrote to him every week—also from her throne—i.e., her bed. No, she wasn't in Kansas anymore with her beloved Richard. With her outings to the Met, Z, at least, was trying to fit in.

Sometimes, Z would sit on the steps before the Met opened, drinking bitter coffee from one of the bright blue disposable cups and people watching for over an hour. The city smelled of a timeless air that came up from the underground subway system, seasoned by the smell of roasted meat and a tinge of rot. Overheard conversations wafted by like snarled music, every grudge taken up and repeated.

Inside, the Great Hall felt like home, a home where she was but one of the yeasty throngs trolling out from the grand entryway. *All of us, moving and branching, nourishing ourselves as Yellow did*—she thought more than once—not on food, but on art and art's obsessions.

Some pieces held more fascination than others. Like visiting the Stations of the Cross before Easter, Z paid tribute to three works on her way to the other rooms: first the Roman copy of a Greek sculpture of the three graces, all headless, yet their marble bodies as supple as if they were alive. She dutifully went to Gallery 162 first, as if Aglaia (Beauty), Euphrosyne (Mirth), and Thalia (Abundance) could engender in her these qualities she had never once felt she possessed. Arms draped across each other's shoulders as if they were one thing, the trio seemed to invite her many sketches of the faces they would have worn.

And then there was Van Gogh's *Cypresses*, the paint so dense and spiraled that Z sat on a bench to the side, observing the canvas's thickness, the fluttering in her heart similar to how she'd felt when she had watched Yellow. Sometimes she doubted that Yellow had happened at all, but when she went to the Met each week, she knew it all was true.

One afternoon as she traced her way back to the entrance through Gallery 810, Z spotted Manet's *The Dead Christ with Angels* for the first time. The graying face on Jesus's cadaver drew her eyes first, then the fretted blue wings of the angel cradling his head. The angel could be male, or it could be female. Its wings were so like faeries' wings.

How had Manet known the lush iridescence of that other world within this one? The word *grace* appeared as if written in rain on her consciousness. The other angel mourned, her bent head in her palm. The first angel, Z realized, looked like Z herself: the dark eyes, the narrow face, the almost masculine nose, lips full. Who was this other as herself? The self she did not know as herself.

The foreshortened Christ's wound was on the wrong side, critics said—a feature that meant the painting had been reviled during Manet's lifetime. Many also thought the painting was near sacrilege—to have made Jesus so human in death.

Each time she stood in front of the painting something new entered her body. *The Kingdom of God is within you*, that is what she remembered Father Beck saying in Mass. But Jesus had been talking to the Pharisees, so Father Beck explained that it was a poor translation. *The Kingdom of God is* ***among*** *you. For only Jesus was God, not mortals, like you or I, and especially not the Pharisees*, he said.

In Manet's painting, she could see that the angels were no longer in the presence of divinity—only its human casing. To Z, it looked like the Kingdom of God was now solely in the angels, not the physical body they attended. Where was this kingdom? Z questioned but did not know.

As Z traced the face of Jesus in her sketchbook with his scrubby small beard, it recalled a face she had always known, its eyes the dimmed eyes of someone she had met or maybe she would meet.

Z's mouth filled with an ecstasy of stars—as if the future were accessible to her in the moment.

oOo

Z often went for lunch at a veggie and yogurt place between classes, walking through nearby Spanish Harlem, passing record stores playing The Clash on high volume. Besides Dot, she hadn't made any friends, and they had different classes anyway. One day at the yogurt place, a man with dark eyes asked if she went to Columbia or Barnard.

Barnard, Z said. They'd been sitting next to each other, eating their white yogurt concoctions in tandem. He told her his name was Gem.

Jim? she asked.

No. He smirked. *Gem. With a* G.

He asked if he could walk with her when she stood up to leave. Something compelled her to him—his sad-eyed Sylvester Stallone look, his arms solid and the shoulders muscled. He wasn't tall, but that didn't matter to Z.

Later, he'd tell her he lifted weights. Later, the two of them standing on his front stoop as a cockatiel in an upstairs window blurted obscenities, he told her he was a writer. He'd gone to Columbia for a while, but the kind of stuff he wrote, he told her, no one was interested in reading.

They laughed me out of class. These days, he said, *I mostly write stories about aliens for the* Enquirer. *I can spin out a few a day.*

He said being a writer meant he spent a lot of time alone. His scuffed-looking studio apartment had a bay window with barbells on the window seat next to a chair full of typed pages. His Selectric typewriter sat on a small table facing the wall.

Z wasn't sure why she gave herself over to this stranger, why she followed him upstairs when he asked and then looked back, almost shyly, to see if she followed. How did she know he was safe?

She wondered about this, until she didn't have the mind to: his glossy head was between her thighs licking her pussy until she screamed aloud. She guessed he was about ten years older than she was. They didn't have intercourse, and later—some years later—she wondered if he'd been on steroids, if the little wild look in his eyes was what came to be known as roid rage.

It was the first time she'd gone that far with a complete stranger. She came in his mouth and thought of Yellow, which was odd because besides her trips to the Met, she thought of them less and less. She remembered the mysterious substance that crept with what looked like all its nerve endings across the fallen log and then down it into a carpet of leaves. With clouds for feet, swirling clouds that grew and took on mass. She came again thinking of Yellow—its erotic reaching.

The stubble on Gem's face scratched the inside of her thighs; the feeling made her come again. In Yellow's presence, Z had sensed not just completeness but a power, something she had forgotten.

Do you believe in aliens? she asked Gem, as she stepped into her underwear, then the worn Levi's she'd bought secondhand. She knew she wouldn't see him again, though he'd torn a piece of newsprint from a pile of discards stacked next to the door and jotted down his phone number. Did the wildness scare Z or his loneliness?

Of course not. He laughed. *I make it all up.* She thought of Yellow again, although thinking wasn't the word for how they had communicated. Words were not adequate. If she told Gem the story of Yellow, he would want to turn it into the kind of *National Enquirer* nastiness that smudged off on your fingers. Looking into the agitation in Gem's mournful eyes, Z realized that she had been going toward this future all along. That the path here was inevitable. That's what Z had learned from Yellow when she was Eliza. But she had forgotten.

oOo

Z's pilgrimage to the Met did not stop suddenly. First there was her work-study job in the Columbia University Library: shelving books and filing cards in the card catalog. She needed more hours, so her work schedule began to push into the weekends, and then she developed the almost overnight friendship with Mikel in her Mysticism class. After that, she was too hungover to go to the Met on Sundays.

She talked to Mikel the first time only a week after she'd had the encounter with Gem. With the irrational idea that maybe she'd willed Gem into existence, could Z will a friend more adventurous than Dot?

For the first three classes, the lanky young man in her Mysticism class had consistently corrected one or the other of the professors who co-taught the class—the stout, Jewish, Asian Studies professor from Barnard, and the hollow-cheeked former Jesuit from Columbia—when they called attendance. Only Columbia classes were co-ed, and Z remained as quiet as she was in her Barnard classes.

Here, but call me Mikel, not Milton, please and thank you. His response always flustered them, and they pecked at the roster like birds.

Mikel sat next to her one day and kicked her army backpack playfully with his foot.

Do you buy everything from the Army Navy Store? he asked, pushing back the hair that fell over his left eye. Like her own, his eyes were heavily lined, his nails painted a dark blue.

Z heard the lilt in his voice, so much like Glen's. She looked down at herself.

Not my pants. They don't make my size, she said.

Oh my god, he said in a staccato, *are you always so serious and, what, southern?* he asked. *MA SIZE? Are you the least bit fun? I can't tell.*

Later, she wondered if she simply decided to rise to his challenge during their every encounter. *Be fun, be fun, be fun*, she reminded herself. They went to the Warehouse District to hear the Dead Kennedys and other upstart bands. She pogoed to the music with the rest of them, wearing a ripped

T-shirt that Mikel had safety-pinned back together artfully. Mikel picked her up when the moshing got too rough, and more than once, Z was sent across the audience on a wave of hands.

They danced together at the grungy side-street gay bars, where often, Mikel told her to get a cab home on her own. *Found someone*, he would wink.

Their drinking—at first bad wine, then bad tequila—would often begin in his dorm room. Their choice of drinks depended on what they could cop from the older students and Mikel's meet-ups. More than once, she woke up in his dorm room on the floor or face-down on the sofa in the common room of her dorm, struggling to remember the previous night's events.

Maybe she stopped going to the Met because her studio art classes were a wash. The art professor never lingered over Z's canvases but only paused briefly, pointing at her wayward strokes. Like her backpack filling with heavy textbooks, her heart was filling with stones.

After Richard dispassionately broke up with her, Dot was a mess at first, and Z invited her out on Saturdays. Dot found plaid skirts and knee socks at Screaming Mimi's, transforming her nerdiness into a look that people gravitated toward. She was a sloppy drunk, though, is what Z thought, but then maybe, so was she. Sometimes, around midnight, someone would get angry, and most of the time, it was Z.

She's so fucking serious, Mikel would constantly say, and Dot would loll her tongue in her mouth and say, *She's just a lil gal from Luziana. Jus leave her alone, Mik.* Z tended to sulk on the subway home, staring at her friends' wisecracking faces. Around their private performance theater, everyone else faded into the background—a gray paste of figures rocking back and forth amid the neon tags that had sprung like electric flowers on the shuddering metal walls as they ratcheted through the dark underworld of New York City.

Z had no talent, she was convinced. And Z didn't know who she was. Had Z also somehow willed people into her life—like Mikel and Dot—who didn't care who she was either?

oOo

Before she'd left his apartment, Z had also torn off a slip of newspaper and handed it to Gem. Watched as he put it in his pocket. Instead of her number, she wrote: *I do believe in aliens. They're all around us.*

oOo

When the Fantasists of the Earth created Skylab, they believed in wonder.

So Clem knew.

They equipped it with the Apollo Telescope Mount, a multi-spectral solar observatory.

All 4,500 pounds to peer into deep space and to peer into the sun. It was an optical telescope, a solar telescope, and a space telescope.

The Fantasists of the Earth equipped Skylab with an orbital workshop, two docking ports, an airlock module with Extravehicular Activity hatches, and gyroscopes to keep it all in spin.

The ATM captured observations made at a variety of wavelengths: x-rays, ultraviolet, and visible light.

Crews did space walks to change the photographic film where cameras captured the earth, the sun, and the specter of space.

When the Fantasists created Skylab, what did they know of the sun?

Clem knew: before Skylab, no one had seen a solar flare, didn't know how the corona of the sun, like the corona of the eye, beheld itself.

How long would each mission be? They didn't know then, but Clem knew now:

Skylab 2, twenty-eight days.

Skylab 3, fifty-nine days.

Skylab 4, eighty-four days.

Skylab orbited Earth 2,476 times during the 171 days and thirteen hours of the three-crewed expeditions, and Clem kept his eyes open in his dark, humid bedroom, trying to look through the ceiling, the roof—and into, into?

Just as he knew the below, he knew the above.

Just as he knew Yellow, he began to know the circulatory powers of Skylab.

Some nights, with his un-twinned twin dozing in the bunk bed below, Clem could see star fire in the dark; Clem could see fleeting asteroids—

Though he'd become the kind of boy who raised his hand too eagerly, though he had become the boy who would tell you facts you didn't need to know, Clem saw into the dark and listened, knew that maybe facts were the fiction.

He knew that one day, he would find the people who would laugh with him at that fact.

Clem knew that the USS New Orleans picked up the last crew on February 8, 1974.

He loved that fact.

He knew, because he understood the Fantasists, that one day, he would live in the beyond.

And beyond that—

Beyond that? Beyond that, Clem, nodding to sleep, began to know. To see how the eye of the sun was the see-er inside him.

After the last crew departed, Skylab became a ghost ship floating over Earth, passing over Australia, six times a day.

NASA made plans to re-inhabit Skylab, then canceled.

When the time came and his twin masturbated in the bunk below him in the dark, sometimes Clem did too, but what he saw was more than a woman, more than a planet—Clem made love to a possibility about knowing Earth's fantasy.

Because of budget priorities, no crews went up to meet Skylab.

And Skylab began to wane, its orbit disintegrating.

Because of the flare activity on the sun's surface that everyone ignored, and because Earth's atmosphere expanded to meet its orbit, Skylab slowed.

The sun's emitted radiation that NASA knew would come every eleven years caused a friction, and Skylab began its plummet.

In the dark heart of his night's bedroom and even in the summer's sun as he followed the tangle of trails to levees behind their house, Clem could feel its decline.

It fell, as all things fall—is what Clem came to know.

The Fantasists of the Earth created Earth time to which Skylab was subject.

Earth time, that's what Pete had said.

Skylab fell out of orbit, sinking into time's spectral hands.

Until the day the ship reentered Earth's atmosphere on July 11, 1979.

Several isolated stargazers in Esperance, Australia watched it scatter into flaming pieces.

Clem came to know that the sonic boom sounded three minutes after those streaking lights in the sky.

NASA thought it would land in the Atlantic Ocean, but one day after impact, they learned that Skylab had littered Australia, had become just debris from a derelict ship.

In the open desert near Esperance, an oxygen tank the size of a car had transformed into a strange extraterrestrial stump, marvelous with a fibrous material that space and fire had made.

They hauled the space stump on the back of a pallet, its wrecked corpse drug around, then laid out for a benefit, where the town of Esperance gathered to look.

The shiny, fibrous space stump made it clear that everything had an ending on Earth.

Some grabbed the loose parts from the space stump and left with them—

When the Fantasists created Skylab, they created Pete Conrad, and they created the orbital workshop where he floated with his crew: *what was up, what was down?*

They created the micrometeoroid shield that had torn away sometime at liftoff, taking one of the panels and jamming one shut.

Clem knew all that.

Though Clem was saddened by Skylab's demise, he understood he'd known it well and had to let it go.

What he wouldn't know was his own course.

Though he ended up valedictorian of his high school.

Though there were girls then who looked at him with stars in their eyes.

He'd be an astronaut, is what Clem thought, a traveler in space.

And he'd go to Tulane on the scholarship he'd earned.

Something inside the see-er in him knew how orbits can decay.

Something inside him, when he entered the girl he thought he would love forever, knew that perhaps she wouldn't always love him back.

Clem knew, and Clem didn't know.

oOo

What are the myths about god? Faith. The exalted? The other? What lived in Z's body was the after-matter of her first rough opening. Every body holds their truth engrained in muscle, tissue, bones. The lake. Power taken from her like a beer can opened, then dispensed.

What are the myths about god? Her desire for others became a forgetting. Was a float out of herself and into the chaos of whatever other presented itself. Everyone had a certain magic. At least for a while.

What are the myths about god? Z went home to New Orleans after graduating from Barnard. Beyond a single dorm room, she could afford nothing in New York City and no lover or friend stuck. In Greenwich Village, she ate her favorite ice cream flavor, Fortune Cookie, and the next day flew home with a trunk and two canvases from her senior year art show. The rest she put in a dumpster behind her dorm. She found an apartment in the Quarter one street away from the French Market. It was small, and she had to share the living room, kitchen, and bath, but it was hers.

What are the myths about god? Z's mother died on the I-10 headed for DC when all her kids were *grown out*, or so she had called it, which meant out of the house. Her twin brothers, Clem and Frank, were freshmen: Clem at Tulane on a scholarship and Frank at LSU to play football. They hadn't strayed far from home. Her mother died brutally, stupidly. She was never a good driver. Clem thought it meant something. Cheryl was angry at Clem for thinking so. Their father became quieter, kept his drunks to himself. Janice lived close enough with her family by that time to bring him food and check on him. After her mother's death, Z took a bus in from the Quarter to watch the Saints games with her father and the rest of the family. Her father was a permanent fixture in the Barcalounger, slamming down beers and po'boys. He didn't pay her any attention, and she hated football. She went less and less.

What are the myths about god? For Z, mourning her mother was a long sleep. She would crawl into her unconscious: rough cuts of dreams within a larger dream. A chewy texture within some larger texture. Years later, after the slow process of grieving, when she was parentless, she realized how free she felt of them. The way parents' expectations impress themselves on you; their failures carried like rocks in your pockets. Years after their deaths, she loved them more than she ever had when they were alive.

oOo

Z's trying to center the canvas on the left rear gallery wall, but it's one of those two-story buildings on Royal Street with a low loft that throws the entire geometry off. Not that Z was ever good at mathematics. She shares her apartment now with Maude, her lover.

Childress stalks past every few minutes, his hands jammed in his black, riveted pants because tomorrow's the opening, and Maude's still at the studio finishing her work. Z could have told him that Maude would push his buttons. At this point in Maude's gallery debut, Z's buttons are jammed all the way in.

Childress stops and glowers at Z, his long frizz of ginger hair swept to one side. He's got multiple piercings—a *multiplicity*, Z muses—in his left ear, his nose, and apparently, both nipples—or so they've been told. *Increases sensitivity when I'm dangling from a rope*, Childress once said.

Where is she? Childress asks, staring at Z, who is perilously close to flying off the ladder.

The canvas's rioting colors have Maude's signature love for minutia. Hidden within the thick splashes of violet are the dark faeries of war drawn delicately with a charcoal pencil. Z can never deny that Maude's talent has always been greater than her own. In this case, she was able to take those beings Z had told her about and translate them into something the world could handle. And appreciate.

Art first, they always said to each other, but Maude really meant it, while Z was gliding on the pure luck of being able to sleep with her and bury her face in Maude's scent. Maude often said that she was still honing her own lovecraft.

You, on the other hand, have your lovecraft down. Better than achieving anything in the art world. I mean a failure in art is not failing at life or anything, Maude said once, tugging down Z's pants and giggling in her ear. Z was a bit stunned that Maude had used the word *failure*. They were both twenty-eight, and it's not like Z had given up.

She'll be here any minute, Z says confidently. When, in fact, she has no idea when Maude will show up, and how. Maude could be as inclement as Nawlins weather: she may be dictatorial and smoldering hot, or sloppy as a two-day bender. It's always a surprise. She'd left Maude clattering among her paint cans, alternately cursing Childress's deadline—*Why does everything have to be done a day before?*—and accusing Z of undermining her.

All I said, Z protested, *was that you may want the paint to dry before hanging.*

Maude's moods, according to Maude, were why she was going to succeed. *How many stable geniuses have you heard about?* Maude asked.

Maude's optically ferocious eyes ringed with dark pencil and her tall angular body, slightly hunched like a walking question mark, pierced Z in some place she'd never understand. Maude hurt her as much as she healed her. Maude's spiky platinum mohawk and thick black chains around her neck—so unlike Z's placid demeanor—gave her the look of a warrior princess. Wasn't that what Yellow said, so many years ago: *one side loves the other?* Without pain, how could there be pleasure?

The doorbell jangles as Maude bangs open the front door.

Childress throws up his hands: *What the living fuck, Maude?* He points to Z. *This cunt can't hang anything.*

Z's holding the wire from both her fingertips, and she thinks of the relief she would feel to simply let it go and kick Childress in his pierced scrotum. Maude doesn't defend her, but at least she remains silent. And, if the two of them are mugging behind her back, Z will stay none the wiser.

I'm open to either of you giving me a hand, Z says breezily, then in a lower voice, *Losers.*

Childress huffs away and Maude says lazily, *I'm on it.* Unlike Z, Maude can easily reach the bottom of the frame, and Z suppresses the rage boiling in the knot of her throat.

At the opening the next night, Z's staring straight at a helmeted fairy, coming at the viewer, surrounded by lush Spanish moss. Maude captured everything Z had told her when she whispered about that night the mysterious forms had taken over her rainy backyard. The first knowledge she had that Yellow had given her some sight—or was it insight?—that no one else had. But she hadn't told Maude about Yellow. Yellow felt sacred and had been difficult to explain. Maybe what Yellow really was would always be a secret between Z and Clem.

The opening is clearly a success. When she overhears the gasps of a couple next to her, Z isn't surprised. *Sold*, Z thinks. Of course, Maude's more talented. Maude may have been right: there's always something in Z that fails her. Her ideas dim before they reach the canvas, or perhaps her execution is too obscure to capture the havoc she cradles between her ribs—day and night, night and day.

You're more into your lovecraft than your actual craft, Maude once said, and, *You're the muse, and I'm the worker.*

But Z works days waitressing, with odd shifts at Kinko's, and weekends hanging small panels of her own sketched faeries on the Jackson Square railing. Her custom sketches of the children of tourists sell better though, so Z's steady income keeps them both afloat. The free time to do art is all Maude's, while the soul-sucking daily work and the inspiration are all Z's.

Though pursued by the *Times-Picayune* reviewer and several buyers all night, Maude makes sure to hook an arm across Z's shoulders. In her artist's talk, she gestures to Z sitting in the front row:

I have my girlfriend Z to thank for sharing her stories, so I can occasionally step into my angel body and create.

Maude's face and body, Z thinks, are monumentally beautiful. *One side loves the other*, she reassures herself.

That night, Z falls into Maude's unfurling petals and finds her taut and generous clit. A knowing pulses through her body. But a terrible thought disarms her: *No, Maude*, she thinks suddenly, *I'm the visionary, and you're the succubus.*

She shakes the feeling off, and so the relationship has to get ugly, as they say, and lasts another two years before Z finds herself—her head newly shaven and her tongue pierced—in Childress's cold garret over Bourbon Street for the night. It would never be clear who left whom.

oOo

What are the myths about god? Z was never a convert, and she was always a convert. The gods came with various sex organs and dark clouds of their own particular drama that they carried, locked in their bodies. After her breakup with Maude, her one true love, mostly she went for the men and women who seemed to wear their wounds on the outside. Like herself. Like Childress who became her lover for a dark season. She never wanted a child and, occasionally, sitting on her humid balcony after a steamy rain, the waterdrops clinging to the balustrades held the reflections of those faeries she saw long ago. The water refracted their tiny faces, their wings closed, and she was certain that what she'd seen at twelve was just one wonder in the biggest wonder. In her daily life, however, all wonders diminished.

What are the myths about god? She wasn't a scholar, or a full-blown, cocksure artist, and maybe she never wanted to be. Maybe she was only meant to be a street artist, known for her rough charcoal sketches of tourist kids. Performance Art had become her thing at Barnard, and she often dreamed up performances but didn't have the guts to see them through.

There was one lucky break: in a five-person show at a small gallery on Chartres Street, she populated a large room with open and empty beer cans—signifying the lake of her body's trauma. Silver and frozen like she'd been when the man had shoved his fingers inside her. She invited ten actors from a nearby theater company to roam the room wearing bedraggled dragonfly wings and Doc Martens. Only two muscular men with tats showed up; they looked mean and effective. On opening night, she led the way as they crushed the cans with their booted feet. The show received a small notice in the *Times-Picayune.*

What are the myths about god? You could say that Clem never recovered. From what, no one was quite sure. But Z blamed herself. A few months after their mother's funeral, Clem dropped out of college. Frank blew out his knee and lost his football scholarship. He didn't return to LSU and got a job on a crew renovating houses.

For a couple of years, Clem roamed out west with friends. When he returned, he worked as a dishwasher at the same seafood joint where she waitressed on Canal. Then he started job-hopping, but he couldn't keep a job or didn't want to. At first, he would land at her apartment on Barracks and Decatur, but most of the time he floated. He had friends around town, he always told her. And, at first, that seemed to be true.

During the day, if she wanted to find him, she discovered his favorite spots. Just around the corner on French Market Place, the shortest block in the Quarter, he met his traveler friends. The ones who rode the trains. He liked to find out where they'd been and tell Z every detail. Some days she'd find him on Royal next to the A&P, sitting on a box wearing the laced black Keds she'd given him, talking to tourists or the Vietnam vets that Clem knew by name.

Everyone in the Quarter loved Clem. He'd grown up to be a tall and beautiful young man with pure eyes, his long hair wound into thick locs that trailed down to his shoulders. His narrow face always wore a sparse, almost delicate beard that he stroked when he talked and that he raised when he laughed. When she looked for him or asked if anyone had seen him, he would always turn up.

Eliza Electric, he'd say when she approached.

Wanna come stay on the couch? she'd ask. Because now it appeared he wasn't staying anywhere.

No, I'm on the trail of this one thought. It's a big one, Eliza, and I'm almost there. His bright eyes would always smile at her though her stomach dropped to see his lips so chafed, almost bruised.

One frigid January morning, when wind came blasting through the streets from the Gulf water, they both walked to the Catholic Mission on Rampart where the intake counselor got Clem a room. When Z checked on him the next week, the counselor said he'd taken off for the bayous or was going to jump a train west. He hadn't yet decided, the young woman said.

Nine months later, he was back in front of the A&P with a mutt that looked like a graying seal next to him on a long rope.

Spare some change for a seeker & his dog? the cardboard sign read, propped in front of him.

Clem jumped up when he saw Z. He reached down to envelop her. In his arms, Z wanted to cry. He'd been gone so long, and now his face was sunburnt, his lips even more bruised.

Electric Eliza! Long time no see. I've traveled the world following the spirit.

What spirit? Z asked. *And how did you leave the country?*

Z never knew, but Clem was panhandling for two people and then two people and one dog. It was the stories former Private Vinnie Gray told Clem that he'd never forget. About lifting the corpses of soldiers from the rice paddies to load onto the choppers. About the give he'd feel when an arm dislocated from the shoulder. That falling away. About not knowing what the faces would look like when they rose from the water. And the time he lost his buddy, David Berkin, MIA, probably killed in action. Until Vinnie died from cirrhosis in 1989, Clem would make sure he found Vinnie—usually near the A&P—to give him half of anything he had. Sometimes cash, sometimes food. If Vinnie wanted a pint, and Clem was flush, he'd get him one.

What are the myths about god? Maude's art became synonymous with the French Quarter. The southern faeries she finely articulated across vivid changing backdrops—alleyways, scrolled balconies, moonscapes, meadows, or gothic trees—captured the Nawlins mood.

Some faeries looked bloodthirsty, some angelic—what were the fae but the beatnik possibility of every person for good or for bad, for lust or for luck? Over a ten-year span, her gallery showings turned into large events in Manhattan. She renovated a historic building on Royal Street adjacent to the botanical garden behind St. Louis Cathedral. Any time of day when Z walked by Maude's Southern Faerie Gallery, the large-paned windows beamed a wicked light.

What are the myths about god? Clem lost track of time. But what was time? When Vinnie's yellowed eyes investigated his own, Clem saw them as clear. Became the amber-brown before Nam. And his own? He had ceased to look at himself.

Brother, everything is going to play out according to God's plan no matter what, Vinnie would say, nodding his head.

Brother, you are right, Clem would say, handing him the pint, or the Styrofoam container, or the wads of wrinkled green paper he'd gathered that day.

We've got to have the faith that everything is as it should be, Vinnie would respond.

Clem said, *I thank you for being my mirror, Vinnie*. He had become the twin that Frank had ceased to be.

oOo

From space, Pete could not see any door, any table, any artifact of the human. And yet, any table could be a door, every thing revolved with everything else. In space, Pete resolved the irony of knowing, the deepening assurance that all was right, that space didn't really hold him. Because . . . space was an immensity, and space was a moment.

From space, the Earth is not a timeline or a points system. It's not a map or a bitter wafer on the tongue. From space, the Earth has no marketing plan or agenda, no electorate, no street signs, no huddled masses yearning to be free.

From space, clouds below scud, they pool and clump; clouds are a murmuration, the sonics of quietude. The oceans carry every shade of blue's infinity. Clouds pink and susurrate like oceans; they soothe and bottom into canyons. The Earth is but a remembrance and a forgetting.

In space, the days were never routine. Strapped into his hammock at night, Pete's dreams were never of the Earth—though from the porthole, he watched its slow revolution.

On Earth, they called him one of the *swashbuckling wisecrackers*: he drove cars fast, wore his suits shiny. He wore the native gap in his teeth—his chin raised in a laugh. On Earth, they called him stupid when he couldn't read and expelled him for the way he was wound. What was good? What was sound? *If you can't be good*, his mother taught him, *Be colorful*. On Earth, he didn't crave love because he had it, and he gave it. On Earth, every laugh he bestowed was a laugh for the eons.

When the shrinks wanted inside his head in those last grueling days as part of the rigorous astronaut trials, he interpreted every inkblot obscene or scatological. Unlike the Mercury Seven ultimately chosen by NASA, he refused the needle to send an electrical jolt into his bones. When the docs wanted a stool sample, he gave it to them in a box with a bow. When they said he wasn't fit for a long-duration flight, he made up his mind to prove them wrong.

On the moon, he became the third man to walk out into that dimension; his laugh rippled back to Mission Control: *Whoopee! It might have been a small one for Neil, but it was a big one for me!* His spacesuit weighed 180 pounds on Earth and thirty pounds on the moon. To him, his spacesuit weighed nothing, in fact.

On the moon, the craters—sprinkled with green and blue dust like glass—were the wells of the self. He had hit his landing: he steered the *Intrepid* to land mere yards away from the *Surveyor,* where it patiently crouched on the moon's surface, left there by the previous mission to monitor space. He also landed fifty feet from the edge of the *Snowman Crater, Ocean of Storms, the moon.* He and Al Bean did two four-hour EVAs—they saw each other reflected in their visors spattered in moondust, like twin boys covered in mud.

And the self couldn't fathom his sheer dumb luck.

In space, when he couldn't dock the module to Skylab, he let loose a string of ripe obscenities. *We've had no fucking connection for eighty minutes.* They'd been up for eighteen hours: docking latches didn't work. They tried every *side-ass goddamned fucking way to lock into place.* He and Astronaut K. made every joke possible about the bad cock not making the join, their voices blasting back through Mission Control and across the radio before someone pushed the off button to radio silence.

In space, Skylab, Day Eight, Pete put on Strauss's *Also sprach Zarathustra,* and they flipped and leaped while the eye of the future watched them rotate in the acrobatics of zero gravity. Pete was the first man to ride a bicycle around the world in ninety minutes as Skylab completed one full orbit.

In space, the gift of weightlessness was everything. Pete remembered always, always tumbling in the womb before he was born and racing to where he wanted to go.

In space, when he and Astronaut K. sprang from the module and the solar array flared open, he laughed the Pete Conrad laugh as he rolled into a soundless infinity . . . *here I am, and there's a yellow stranger.* Above, below, what was slow in his own revolutions touched him everywhere. There was yellow, the yellow hand, the yellow thumb. A beautiful emergence, co-existing with This.

As if, Pete laughed, *as if . . .*

In space, the self was weightless and to go all the way to the end of the umbilical was to go to the beginning of pure thought, to the beginning of a one-celled organism that was all of it—is All: no Pete, no Yellow, all Pete, all Yellow.

oOo

Z had forgotten until Clem reminded her. About meeting the astronaut. He'd saved the news clipping about the astronaut's death and tucked it within the tongue of his shoe. She thought it ingenious the way Clem seemed to find places for things when he had nothing. And by this time, he wanted nothing.

It was the year 1999. Clem was thirty-four. Two years before the nation would be broken by four planes ripping through the sky and into America's icons: the Twin Towers, the huddled shell of the Pentagon.

That day, she found Clem where she often found him: at the port in New Orleans, feeding seagulls with a discarded loaf of French bread. He would eat a few handfuls and then hold out the crusts so that the gulls would swoop down to take them from his raised palm. The gulls floated over him, shifting for dominance.

Heading down the steps to the park bench where his sleeping bag lay coiled like a spent chrysalis, she saw his figure backdropped by the early sun. He looked like a master puppeteer. Was he holding some unseen strings so that the dozen or so gulls sprang from his hands like a flock of holy ghosts, or were they the puppeteers animating the broadly smiling man who fed them?

Electric Eliza! Come! he said. She couldn't help joining him in his daily ritual of feeding the gulls. Z did love the way that as they came closer, bravely levitating just a foot or so from her outstretched hand, their beaded eyes looked directly into her own: calculating distance, but also, with a kind of knowing.

Yes, it seemed that they knew, even more than she did. When she admitted what she thought, Clem said, *Of course, Z. They know because you know.*

It was the kind of gibberish that made Z feel so helpless. He wasn't getting any mental health counseling once he was firmly classified not just as a drifter, in and out of temporary housing, but as a street person. By late July, the pavement heated up, hot enough for the egg trick, but Clem still stood barefoot, his sneakers laced together on the park bench. His feet looked puffy and blackened. His soles probably hard as rocks.

He died, Z! In the most amazing way!

Who died? Z asked.

Pete, of course. Our Pete.

I don't know who you mean, Clem. Are you sleeping out here now?

He shrugged. *Sometimes. Remember going to the Superdome when we were kids and the way you saw Pete first? Went straight up to him?*

She'd almost gotten used to Clem's smells: his soiled clothes, rangy Gulf waters, often the whiff of urine, sometimes weed. All mixed with the dense tarragon smell that was Clem to her. Would always be Clem.

Then she did remember the Superdome. His eyes went soft when she smiled.

Oh, yeah. Pete, she said.

They'd bussed kids into the Superdome from many of the New Orleans parish to see the astronauts who would each talk about Skylab and their trip into space. The event had only fueled Clem's obsession with NASA and all the space missions.

But she and Clem had missed the early bus heading to the Superdome. They ran back home, breathless and dropping their satchels on the floor. Their mother slammed the door shut after them, puffing furiously on her cigarette. She woke up their still-sleeping father and told him to get the kids to *some extracurricular thing clear 'cross town.* Because their father kept his own hours at his struggling insurance business, he drove them to the Superdome, braking hard at stoplights, launching them forward, and muttering at the other cars moving lazily in the muggy heat.

Ya think they'll be wearing their spacesuits, Clem? their father asked, dead serious. Clem responded in kind, moving forward in the front seat until his lap belt pulled him back.

Dad, do you really think they will? I mean they weigh over one hundred pounds!

Well, who knows, Clem? But Z heard his thickly lacquered put-down voice. *Maybe they will. They could take a dump in there, and we'd never know!* From the backseat, Z watched Clem's head go still.

Every homeroom teacher nominated one girl and one boy from each grade. She knew why his second-grade teacher chose Clem: he had always been the smartest in the class, and he'd written a report on Skylab as soon as he got the chance.

But why me? Z wondered. It was her last year at St. Catherine, seventh grade, and the only thing that made sense was that all the other girls had talked about how boring and stupid it would be. *Childish,* she heard one say from their huddled group.

Or maybe Z's art teacher had told her homeroom teacher about the picture she'd drawn for Clem. The assignment was to draw a picture of anything in the news. Clem's constant chatter prompted her to use the charcoal sticks poised in a small box at the rear of the classroom to shade an expansive dark space and to tether one long ribbon outside the picture. She used a yellow marker to color the ribbon just for Clem. At the other end of the ribbon was one tiny astronaut. *Spacewalk*, she titled it.

So there they were, just going through the turnstile, with kids and teachers hurrying to their seats and their father red-faced, dripping wet in his work suit in the early September heat. Almost growling like a bear and Clem saying, *I have to go to the bathroom, Daddy*, and their father saying: *Christ, Clem. Can't you wait? We still have to find your school's section.*

Clem practically held himself. Z had to go too but knew not to make another request of her father.

H-E-double hockey sticks! Get your butt in that restroom and get back out here faster than you can shake two nickels together.

I'm going too, Z said, and ran before he could fuss her out. Z sighed with relief once she got in the stall, pulled down her sweaty tights, and let it rip. She heard girls in the other stalls, the doors banging closed, and a band out on the field playing *When the Saints Go Marching In* with trumpets wailing.

She washed her hands quickly, looking at the strange girl wearing a dark pixie cut, her mouth one grim line. Since her encounter with the man at the lake, sometimes the image of herself seemed to come away in the mirror. As if the girl in the mirror might walk off, leaving the real Z standing there, wishing she had a body again.

As she ran out, she saw the kicked-up heels of other kids running too, and the back of her father, his shoulder against the wall. His nearly-bald head didn't look as shiny from the back and his suit wasn't as crumpled as she'd thought.

Z had a sudden feeling of gratitude for her father. Here they were, ready to see the astronauts, and he'd taken her and Clem, not his favorites. Not Cheryl, not Frank. She skipped towards her father, her heart lifting, and took his hand. It was smooth and firm, and, for a second, the hand stiffened.

When she looked up, expecting to see her father's face, there was another's. He had a gap between his teeth, and his eyes seemed to light and dance when he saw her. Before she could pull her hand away, he said, *Hello there.*

I'm sorry, Z said, thinking she should be afraid, but he was nothing like the man at the lake.

Instead, his grin widened, and he cocked his head as Clem came running up to them.

Aren't you—? Clem asked.

The man patted Z's hand and then crouched so that he was eye level to Clem.

I'm Pete. What are your names?

It's you! It's you! Clem hopped towards Pete like he was ready to launch.

Do I know you, little man? Pete joked.

I'm Clem, and this is my sister Eliza. What was the moon like? And space? And Skylab?

The entire day came back like a wistful dream as she stared at the wrinkled newsprint, the squawk of seagulls ringing. The obituary headline: *Pete Conrad Dies.*

Why are you happy that he died, Clem? Z asked. *And in a motorcycle accident?*

Only way to go, don't you think, Eliza? I mean you walk on the moon, and you go through the sun, and you find Yellow. What the living fuck. Go out in style! Clem leapt up on the bench, just as he would have when he was eight.

Z wanted to weep then, thinking that meeting that one kindly man, albeit a famous one, only served to solidify Clem's obsessions.

She'd already told Clem the lie that if he hurt Yellow, her mother's life was at risk. And their mother had died when Clem was just eighteen. Could she ever take back such a curse?

Now, he stood on the bench looking down at her. *Come on, Eliza; you felt it too, didn't you? We knew each other—we all recognized each other.* He grabbed at the air for emphasis. Z looked up into his beautiful face, though it was always sunburned now. He was aging before his time. She told her second lie to Clem because she couldn't support his madness anymore. She'd started it all, and why continue? Clem had to land; that's all Z knew.

So she said, *No, no, Clem. Recognize him? I just took his hand because I thought he was Dad.*

You knew we were all connected, Clem said, dropping his arms to hang loosely.

Okay, I'm not saying he wasn't a nice guy, but why wouldn't he be? We were just kids.

Clem appeared unswayed. *You know what Yellow means, and I know what Yellow means. And so did he. He left clues everywhere. Read down here. Look what Pete said when someone asked him about life in space. Read it aloud.*

Z looked down at the newsprint going smeary with use.

There's plenty of unearthly things moving around in my refrigerator. So, there's always a chance of life springing up anywhere, she read.

See? Clem said. *The guy's a genius and funny as fuck. Life springing up anywhere. Like Yellow! The big mind, baby!*

He turned from her, began clapping and swaying. He sang *Lucy in the Sky with Diamonds.*

Oh, shit, Clem. Are you tripping right now?

Clem launched into an even louder version of *I Am the Walrus*, floating his arms and stomping his feet on the bench. His voice rose into the wind over the Gulf waters. A group of tourists went by, and two teenagers turned back, pointing at Clem and laughing. Z saw him as they did. The Bird Man of New Orleans. A crazy aging hippie singing nonsense.

He sat down on the bench. *Hell, no, Electric*, he said, soberly. *It's just that I wish you weren't so lost.*

It was one of the many conversations they would have that confused her. And little did she know then that Clem had only six years left.

In Earth time, at least.

Earth time. When he bent and held their hands, with Clem bouncing beside him like a jackrabbit, Pete had used those words.

The moon was incredible, Pete had answered Clem, looking straight into his eyes. He turned to Z. *Like living in the best movie of your life. Like being in a dream you never want to wake up from. But you don't have to wake up, you just live it full-on. I'm happy to see you both, in Earth time anyway!*

The flash of his grin, the quick squeeze of their hands. Their father came hurtling up behind the three of them. Pete's disappearance was almost magical. He would reappear on stage with the other two astronauts not much later. The children-filled stadium would hear each of them talk through the loudspeakers about being on Skylab: their revolutions around the Earth, the experiments they did. But there was a delay to their words, as remote as if they were still in space.

Yellow was gone by then too. Their Yellow was no more. Or were they?

But that was just in Earth time. And yes, she felt she knew Pete, recognized him as her own. But by then, Z had only her lies to keep her safe.

oOo

Pete can sense it before it's upon him. Not trepidation, he can't call it that. Instead, he feels it as both an absence and a presence, somewhere just near his heart like an empty room that will soon be filled with what he could only just begin to see.

He feels it when he makes the plans to ride from his home in Huntington Beach north to Monterey with Don and his grown son, Alan. They'll bring a few friends with them.

When he gets off the phone with Don, he feels it, stuck between his ribs—that empty room and its possibility. It's there when he puts on his leathers; it's there even in Nancy's echoing smile as she watches him strap his helmet on, waving as she turns back at the garage door to go inside.

They'll go north. Maybe it's just a sense of freedom—the body's ideas, he knows, are limited: concrete and conditional. But the spirit—one reason that he rides fast, one reason that compels him to drive the road like he tripped across the moon. *Whoopee*—he said then, kicking the regolith—coated in moondust, in asteroid dust. Damn, you name it—he's always been a spirit in life's crater. The porous median between this and that—endless space and endless dimensions—something he can almost smudge. Something he can almost trip across.

He rides in a tight group with Don and the rest until he senses something more: the dark tar mirage of the road urging him toward something. Some would call it completion; he has no name for it yet.

On his spacewalk repair of the solar shield, no one saw him go through Yellow. But no one could contradict it either. He knows he had entered and passed through a stranger. The yellow he'd seen again out the viewport of Gemini 11—orbs within some bigger protean shape, big as a stadium and immense with light.

He breaks from the small cluster of cycles after their lunch in Ojai. On Highway 150, he feels the syncopated roll of the road, taking the turns, the low-crowned oaks hovering sometimes overhead and sometimes nearby;

the browned and rolling hills like a balm below the power of his bike: every movement a movement that grace allows. His son's face drifts in—Christopher. Only twenty-nine, he died nine years ago. His last few breaths with lymphoma, discovered too late to do anything useful. His pale lips, and how Pete had crawled up next to him in the bed, clutching his first wife's hand. The triad of them—another magical three—Christopher, Jane, and Pete. Just like the three in space: Kerwin, Weitz, and Pete made three.

They held hands, pulsing together as the machines slowed. Christopher's throat clattered for breath for more than twenty long minutes before the sudden startle of his eyelids opened like a curtain raised.

Christopher's eyes were brown, but in them Pete saw Earth, the blue oceans, saw him look at the empty space with awe—so Pete takes that hairpin curve fast, twisting the throttle; as the engine hums, radiating up his spine, he sees an endless road, gravel on the turn like his memories of moondust manifested it; he feels the slow spin of his tires trying for traction and veers toward the ditch across the yellow line as he hurls across it, so that in every nerve, Yellow circles and spirals, advancing as the bike goes under him, his legs clutching until they can't anymore and he flies off, his body launched into an infinite sky; Pete feels just as he did when he came to the end of that umbilical—a sonic freedom of the spirit jettisoning out to meet itself.

Yes, is how he hears it, entering Yellow for a few minutes, just the way he had popping off the fuselage of Skylab.

Yes, his body skids and slides across the pavement.

And yes, after the initial shock, he lies still. Still grinning, though, thinking *what a ride, what a ride*. Even as he hears a bike stop, sees Don's face drained of color, hanging over his own, then the sound of all the other bikes braking around him.

What a ride, he says, standing, even though his friends scream, *Don't stand*, and his insides burn. He retreats back to the pavement still wearing his stunned grin. There's the ambulance siren and the EMTs now on him and everything slightly jumbled. They load him in. Even though he protests *I'm fine, I'm fine*, Pete can't keep still. His breathing's rough and even though merciful hands are on him, and his heart's beating strong, he looks at the useless machines and thinks of space's hands, remembers holding up his giant gloved clown-hand on the moon and laughing. And for the sake of everyone, including this myth of himself, he's laughing now.

Hands, he thinks, *how funny!* He holds up his own, but they're bloodied, and once they get to the hospital, they say he's in shock.

For Chrissakes, it's okay! he roars. His friends have told the docs who he is, and now there's more of them gathered around. But what are they going to do with the air beginning to fill his chest cavity, creating an uninhabitable room? Their attention is still both urgent and careful, but that sense he had this morning just keeps growing, multiplying and adding with all the raw details of the inevitable. To ease the pain, Pete's got stories.

He tells them about that damn eyebolt out Skylab's left rear port sitting right there for no good goddamn reason, except to give them a little leverage in a weightless universe.

When that damn hinge breaks, we're thrown end over end.

They're nodding and smiling, but their eyebrows are drawn in with concern. *You wouldn't believe the exhilaration!* he says, then thinks better of it. *Oh yeah, you will. You all will!*

His ribs are on fire, and his breathing is rough. By that time, they have escorted Nancy in, her face spotty and washed with tears. He takes her shaking hands, telling her it's all going to be fine.

He asks the doc's masked face hovering over him: *You ever been on the moon?*

No, sir.

But you will. You will!

Nancy's crying, and he sees the fear mounting in her face. The feeling like glass crackling in his chest makes everything difficult.

Gimme, he says, grabbing her hand. *What a ride, right? Remember I told you about Christopher?* She's nodding her head and crying. *That last look? His eyes seeing it all?* Her brows draw in.

Yes, yes, her stuttering reply.

That's it. It's all there, Nancy.

He turns his face away from the human and into the strong yellow orbs glaring from the ceiling.

It's that sense again of real weightlessness occupying not just his mind but every pore of him. Before long, he knows he's going to take his last roll right to the end of his being.

He wants to feel what it means to touch one last time, and so he clutches Nancy's hand in his own—warmth, and then nothing to leverage against, just one final catapult up, and consciousness drifting, merging, meeting itself to know itself.

Oh, the eternal, someone says. Was it him? He laughs the Pete Conrad laugh, one more time.

oOo

You might say it's coincidental that *Ojai* means moon in Native American Chumash language.

That Pete took his final ride in Ojai, California.

That the fingernail half-moon floated in the wide blue skies on the day he died, July 8, 1999.

Quantum entanglement says:

> Everything is energy.
> Energy connects everything.
> Energy carries information.
> The past, present, and future all exist simultaneously.

In the moon's eye, Pete takes flight.

In the moon's eye, Einstein shambles along the streets in Princeton, New Jersey.

Reality is merely an illusion, albeit a very persistent one, Einstein said.

oOo

Katrina Timeline

Friday, August 26, 2005:

Saints pre-season game at the Superdome;
they are bested by the Baltimore Ravens
That night, Hurricane Katrina crosses over the southern tip of Florida,
a Category 1 storm, and enters the Gulf of Mexico overnight, with
maximum winds of 75 mph

5:00 p.m.: The National Hurricane Center adjusts the possible path from
Florida Panhandle to the Mississippi/Alabama coast
Governor Kathleen Blanco declares a state of emergency
for the state of Louisiana

Saturday, August 27:

5:00 a.m.: Hurricane Katrina cycles up to a Category 3 intensity

5:00 p.m.: New Orleans mayor Ray Nagin requests voluntary
evacuation of New Orleans metropolitan area residents

Sunday, August 28:

7:00 a.m.: Katrina forms into a Category 5 storm with winds
exceeding 160–175 mph over the Gulf of Mexico's warm waters

9:30 a.m.: Blanco and Nagin order mandatory evacuation for
New Orleans residents; the Superdome is listed as a "refuge of last re-
sort"; 100,000 people did not or could not leave the city

By the afternoon, the National Weather Service warns that the levees could be breached

25,000–30,000 people take shelter in the Superdome

Monday, August 29:

6:10 a.m.: Katrina makes landfall with Category 3 winds—up to 129 mph and 170 miles wide

9:00 a.m.: Levee breached in Lower Ninth Ward flooding eastern New Orleans

Thousands of people trapped on rooftops—parts of French Quarter remain dry

Tuesday, August 30:

80 percent of New Orleans is covered in water as high as 20 feet

Industrial canals breached

200,000 homes are submerged while in over 90-degree heat

The city is without power, drinking water, or communications; Looting begins

Wednesday, August 31:

Water levels are equalized between Lake Pontchartrain and New Orleans

Rescue crews try to get to homes; most are stranded because of limited or no communications

The Cajun Navy—a volunteer force—rescues about 1,500 people

At the Superdome, where 35,000 people are stranded, anarchy and rapes are reported as drinking water and food declines

Bloated bodies float in floodwaters

September 28, 2005:

1.3 million citizens from the New Orleans population are dispersed in all fifty states

November 21, 2005:

Estimated death toll is 1,300–1,500

Yet other sources say that 6,644 people are still unaccounted for, 1,000 of them children

oOo

A year after Clem died, or—more accurately—a year after he was still lost to her, Z was living in Atlanta, partly in exile from the city ravaged by Hurricane Katrina, partly because returning home would bring on all the ammunition of her own self-blame.

The Federal Emergency Management Agency had given Katrina survivors stipends for rent, which in Z's case, she handed over every month to Cheryl's husband, Jim. Her sister and brother-in-law drove away from their mini-mansion in the suburbs of Atlanta at 5:30 a.m. every weekday, taking turns towing their two towheaded kids in one or the other minivan to a private school nearer to their workplaces in downtown Atlanta. Getting there, traversing the city's octopus-like freeways, often bumper-to-bumper, took over an hour each way. Unlike Janice, who had popped out three kids by the time she was twenty-five, Cheryl had waited until she had found a well-paying job in a prominent accounting firm and a husband who had done the same before starting a family.

Z seldom joined the family upstairs; instead, she occupied the mother-in-law suite in the basement, often making her meals there. Z overheard Cheryl call her *my freaked-out artist sister* on the phone. The thin drywall of the cavernous house conducted sound quite perfectly downstairs. Or maybe it was Cheryl's voice, so much like their mother's but with a wheedling tone their mother had never used. When either of her children, Ashley or Winston, began to whine about something, Cheryl presented each of them with *options*.

Since the blue bowl is dirty, she heard Cheryl asking, *then what about the red?* But the red was never a good option, and Cheryl was harried, already worn down and too thin in her business suit. Z heard her washing the blue bowl while Jim asked for more coffee.

For the past year, Z had worked as a visiting artist in the Atlanta public schools three to four days a week. Her *Tales from the Flood*, a multimedia installation, had caught the fancy of the city art council's administrators, *multimedia* being a catchphrase they knew would capture the respect of urban high schoolers. Z had spliced together footage from the news along with the audio tapes she had recorded on Sunday, August 28, the day after Mayor Nagin had merely suggested that it would be a good idea to evacuate New Orleans. The day she went looking for Clem.

Before the eye of the hurricane held them in its gaze, the city had a surreal quality. On Saturday, the Quarter streets, absent of the tourists, were still chock-full of the locals—no one seemed to take the news too seriously. The weather had cooled and a voluntary evacuation hardly registered, especially since the night before the entire city, in typical Saints fashion, had either gone to the Superdome or, like her father, sat glued to their television sets, enthralled. After all, just the day before Lady Katrina had wound down to a Category 1, right?

Now, she wondered why she hadn't insisted Clem stay with her when she'd found him on Saturday. The night when the storm started to sound more menacing than they'd expected. She had discovered him near the LaTrobe Fountain, at the tail-end of the French Market, and he sat on one of the benches listening to two buskers—one on a sax and one using his drumsticks on an overturned plastic bin.

Hey, come stay the night on the couch, Clem, she'd said, but he only smiled up at her. He was keeping time to the music with that funny stick with a pinecone on top—an affectation that made him appear to be some kind of ludicrous royalty around the Quarter.

No need, Electric, he'd said.

But there's a hurricane coming. Z hoped her tone was urgent yet wouldn't drive him further into himself. She sat down on the bench next to him. The drummer looked like a boy of about fifteen. And the sax player? Maybe his father. A short-legged mutt with graying whiskers sat in front of Z, leaning into Z's strokes.

Aren't they good? Clem had said, nodding at the musicians. Z felt impatient. She looked out at the Gulf but saw there were no ships on the water: only one rocking ferry, and she should have seen it as a signal of what was to come.

It would make me feel better if you came back with me, was her last shot.

And Clem did a funny thing then; he didn't even look her way at all, watching instead the father and son with a bemused smile. But he cradled her hand. All she could think was how big and rough it felt. He kept time with a thumb on her knuckles and said, *There's no need to succeed, Z. Okay? Remember that.*

Z shook his hand off and stood up. *I'm not talking about succeeding. I'm talking about being safe from the storm.*

Hey. Clem caught her hand as she was turning away. *It's not your fault about Mama, Eliza. I never thought it was.* Then he abruptly asked: *You know what they're playing?*

What did you say? Later, she wondered if she'd heard him right. He still hadn't looked her in the eyes. *Clem, no, I don't know what they're playing. But wait, tell me more about Mama?*

A Love Supreme, he said, squeezing her hand. With his other hand, he lifted the stick with the funny pinecone on the end and lowered it to the ground in front of the jazz duo, as if knighting them.

Z stalked off, her chest feeling snarled with cotton. She glanced back at Clem's quiet profile, thinking she'd come by again the next day. Thinking that maybe the hurricane would veer off again, as it had done already, glancing Florida, yes, but then moving back out to sea.

When she went looking the entire next day, she couldn't find him, so she'd taken the handheld recorder and asked all the street kids and regulars if they'd seen him. The stories they told grew more varied and fantastical as she ventured further into the Quarter.

The voices were slurred, or they were gruff Nawlins voices.

Saw Clem couple hours ago, you know, grinning ear to ear. Told me: This moment is the exit without the sign, said the sax player. His son was crouched over the short-legged mutt she'd seen before, feeding him from the box of leftovers Z had brought with her.

The exit without the sign, Z repeated.

The sax player's voice was full and throaty. *Damn, sometimes I could follow that man, but most of the time his words were lost on me.*

You two have a place to stay? Z asked, as she had asked every one of them.

Buses out of town at the Superdome, he'd said. *Heading there now.* Only later did Z find out that the buses were figments. Only later did she find out that it was possible that over one thousand children were among the dead and unrecovered. Only later did she wonder about the boy who did the drumming, his father, and the short-legged dog.

Near Jackson Square, Beatrice, the woman always cloaked in garbage bags, said Clem told her he wasn't going to the Superdome. *Old Clem said it was going to be like Noah's flood, and did I have any jaguars with me.*

He said what? Whenever she played the recording back, she heard her own disbelief.

The woman repeated what he said, then eyed Z with suspicion. *I don't have any jaguars.*

There was no time. She had to meet Frank at her apartment after he'd picked up her father in Metairie. They'd heard traffic was backed up for hours. She'd been in charge of Clem, and she'd failed.

Beatrice refused Z's offer of a ride.

On her way back to her apartment, she'd stopped on the shortest street—French Market Place—and looked for and found Douglas, the young man who'd been honorably discharged from his service in Iraq. *Can't get a foothold, that's all,* Clem once said about him. Douglas had gone AWOL when the torture started at Abu Ghraib. His face beamed when Z asked after Clem.

Since all the ships had gone out, I could see clear across the harbor, Douglas shouted. It was evening by then, the squalls had started, and she and Douglas held on to the iron bars on the closed-up shop door. She could barely take in what he said next: *I swear I saw him walking across the Mississippi on his bare feet, just like an angel. Heading for the ferry.*

That ferry? Z scanned the bay and saw the large craft roiling on the water.

Yeah, but it was further out this afternoon, I reckon, heading somewhere. Douglas's teeth chattered, even though it was swelteringly humid, and Z had the urge to hug him to her because maybe he was the last person to see Clem. Even if everything else were only Douglas's figments, something about Clem still gave him joy. He declined her offer to leave New Orleans with her family. *Guess I'll stay, been good to me, Nawlins.*

In her media installation, Z projected Weather Service footage from outer space of the hurricane—the eyewall swollen around what looked like a void. It was no figment, and the next morning while their car had crawled up I-10 along with everyone else's, her father and Frank badgering each other the entire way, the water was breaking through the levees, the water swarmed the streets, swirled and choked off the estuaries, the water took down centuries-old water tupelos, the water upended their mother's coffin in the graveyard in Metairie. The water was a force that entered her dreams.

She didn't say who Clem was in her art installation. Sometimes you had to spare the viewer from the crippling truth of loss. While her sister and her family went about their comfortable life upstairs, Z often lit a joint in the downstairs bathroom with the exhaust fan on. It happened sometimes that

Clem would visit her, usually when she discovered herself sobbing on the bath mat with her head turned to the left and there he was, sometimes disguised as a small rabbit and sometimes a grasshopper. But most of the time, she just heard him breathing next to her, and she caught the solar flash of his wheat-colored locs, his blindingly white teeth. She wondered about the exit with no sign. She wondered if she'd made up what he said. Had he never blamed her for their mother's death? Why had she said such a thing when they were only children?

She wondered about that stick with the pinecone on the end, and what Clem could see that she couldn't.

oOo

Z was at a house party in Atlanta, higher and more talkative than she would've liked among so many people she'd just met. They were mostly Jilly's friends. Jilly of the moon-face and pouty lips. The intent gaze. Poor Jilly that Z had begun to detest. She even had an itemized list in her mind of where they'd gone wrong.

The party was their breaking point. If they hadn't gone, what would have happened? Looking back, Z could say maybe she needed an excuse to leave Jilly. They sat around holding craft beer bottles and finger-smudged wine glasses in a house in Grant Park. A summer night with insects throbbing outside. Hurricane Katrina came up and Jilly said, *Z was there, right, Z?*

Z was thinking of the thousands of unrecovered bodies, but she wasn't going to talk about looking for Clem. The storm just starting to come inland as she trudged the barren Quarter streets and the homeless she'd talked to, holding garbage bags and cardboard boxes over their heads. Elated, many of them, like this was the best damn adventure.

Instead, the somewhat ragged floral wallpaper in the Grant Park house reminded her of going back to Metairie on September 5. It was the first day they were all allowed to go back to Jefferson Parish, back to the house they'd grown up in. The house's walls were thick with blackening mold. She could barely see the traces of her mother's old wallpaper, a geometric pattern in those burnt oranges and golds of the '70s. So, she told Jilly's friends about it. There were about seven guests left: cross-legged on the floor and perched on the sagging sofa where Z sat. She talked to them as if they could ever inhabit the sunken-chest feeling of her remorse. The dearth and depth of it. Of course they couldn't know.

It was just a party story to them, their eyes rapt as she described the overturned corduroy Barcalounger that her father had lived in for most of his adult life in that house. Detritus on the floor thick with a black sludge.

Look at this, she'd said to Clem, and they both smiled as she turned over the cheap gold frames with their school pictures. In the one of the entire family, taken at JCPenney, the floodwaters had saturated the colors and the mold spotted their faces with a blot of darkening spores. It felt good to rip it up.

Clem laughed. His locs like that halo of light he always wore. Only his smile kept her going. He kicked the Barcalounger.

Take that, you bullying fucker.

That's good, Z said. Her father was still living with Frank in Shreveport where they'd fled. He didn't much care to talk on the phone, and truth be told, he didn't much care for Z or Clem.

Guess we're too different, Z said aloud and kicked the Barcalounger too. Maybe she'd kicked so hard that her foot hurt, but she wasn't sure.

Yeah, and so what? Clem cocked his head a little to his left in that way he had, wearing a sly grin.

Yeah, and so what? Z echoed back.

It was good to be with him again. Z didn't tell the house party crowd about going out back with Clem, about seeing the clotted junk-filled space where the plum tree had been. She only knew where they were because of the leaning black gum tree. She was disoriented, but Clem wasn't. He sat on a tangle of crap from nearby houses that had washed up against their sunken back fence.

Remember the faeries? Clem asked.

You saw them too?

Of course I did. Clem said, putting a hand on Z's shoulder as she bent to weep. His firm touch brought back the feeling of Yellow in her chest.

Yellow's not dead. Don't worry, Z. Remember—they're immortal.

I know, she shuddered. *But where?* she asked Clem. His eyelids were slightly lowered, the blue eyes her very sky.

Everywhere. Everywhere.

Her mind floated back to the party. All eyes were on her, though most were at half-mast. Three empty wine bottles on the table and the back throb of Fiona Apple. A slim man stroked his hipster beard. *Awesome story, man. I mean you and your brother made it through all that. Can't even imagine.*

Me neither, Jilly smirked. *Since I thought your brother died in the hurricane.*

Z turned to her, her head made slow by the high or the beer or the relationship. She blinked. She was right. Clem couldn't have been there. Her first thought was to strike Jilly's complacent face. But she swallowed.

He did die in the hurricane. Or he's been lost in the hurricane. MIA.

What's that supposed to mean? Jilly said. Maybe Jilly was too young to know what it meant.

MIA. Missing in Action. She thought of her MIA bracelet listing David D. Berkin. It had been carried away by the hurricane, of course. Maybe it had spun through the air and out into the Gulf.

There was a long silence, and she knew they were all watching her. Of course, Clem was dead. But they had never found his body, and the day she'd returned to the house, he'd been there all along. Hadn't he?

Z managed a laugh and said to Jilly: *I told it that way just so you could make me feel like a fool.*

No one knew what to say, or at least that's what Jilly's tear-puffed face said to Z later.

You are massively uninteresting, is one thing Z remembers saying as she packed up her things and left the cat hair-bathed apartment on Ponce where she and Jilly had lived together for a little over a year.

Z could see how hateful she'd been only now. Jilly was just telling the truth. Or the truth as she knew it.

Things like that caught her up now and then. Ideas of immortality. In the depths of her being, she knew Clem wasn't a ghost because they were all ghosts—every one of them.

oOo

A few years after Z moved back to New Orleans, she's standing in the small and over-curated bookstore on Pirate's Alley when Childress strides in. Z feels caught with a hook in her mouth. Open before her on the stacked book table labeled "Local Authors" is Maude's most recent monograph. Titled *Southern Faeries*, and published, she's already noted, by one of the best art publishing companies in New York.

Z! Look at you checking on Maude's success. He's wearing his newest affectation, the colorful sherbet plaid shirt and a neon-green seersucker suit. He's still got a few of the piercings left in his ear, but the ginger hair is about gone. Looks like he shaves what little he has and lets his beard gloss with a five-o'clock shadow. *When did you get back in town?*

It's the question the old regulars ask each other. Some never returned, and some, like Childress, have reinvented themselves, post-Katrina. He's refashioned his art space by adding an artisanal whiskey bar.

Z probably has not changed much; at least, not at first glance. Z sighs, closing the book.

Does it matter? she says. Post-Katrina, she just keeps speaking her mind.

Childress holds a hand to his mouth in mock horror. *You bitch*, he says. *I've missed you.*

But Z hasn't missed Childress. The two years in his drafty garret were when she'd become vulgar, even to herself. When, adrift and broken open from the breakup with Maude, she'd given herself over, entirely, to Childress and his sadism.

That fact has always been apparent between them.

How about that? Z says. Something her mother would have said.

You bitch! he says again. *Okay, let's just talk about this high and mighty sloth creature*, Childress says, fingering the monograph. The faeries on the cover are new—looking more fragmented and abstract than the careful charcoal faeries floating in the tendrils of Spanish moss that she got famous for. Childress's art show launched Maude Bileski's faerie figures which had become ubiquitous with New Orleans. She screwed Childress by going with a bigger gallery in New York City, when given the chance.

These are very interesting, Z says. *I mean, she's always upping the ante on them.* These new faeries Maude had painted with frail brushstrokes against ice-encased black tree limbs.

She's a sloth; she stole them from you. We both know that. Childress still has that same scent that she remembers from the times they'd fucked each other. A pungent mint-lemon trying to cover the smell of his burning. He'd liked spanking her hard with a paddle; he liked dressing up. He liked nipple clamps on both of them. He liked frothing at the mouth and spitting on her, and at the time, Z didn't think she deserved tenderness. She'd only quit when he brought in Marlowe. The grinding hurt, feeling suffocated between the two of them. She used the safe word almost immediately and moved out the next day. One obvious step for most people, a huge leap in maturity for Z.

Z rifles through the pages. *Look*, she says. *These are all new. These are entirely Maude's. They are exquisite.*

She's got talent, but so do you.

How do you know? Z muses, turning the book over to read the back cover blurbs, and she realizes that for once, Childress has gone quiet. She doesn't look up at him. It tires her to think why she thought she needed punishing. It tires her to realize that Childress had been a version of her punishing father.

I saw your multimedia show on Katrina. It was powerful. You've got something, always have. Who were you looking for?

I lost my brother Clem in Katrina, Z says, and she's surprised by Childress's freckled hand on her upper arm.

Oh, everyone loved Clem! He waits a few beats, his hand tightening. *I lost both my parents. My mother in that hellhole nursing home where they decided who lived and died, and my father had a stroke in the heat two days after the flood.*

Z looks up at him, and he juts out his chin, avoiding her eyes. *Who could get to him through that mess?* he said.

I'm sorry, she says, putting a hand over his hand.

Yeah, we're all sorry for each other, he replies, but they keep their hands there and Z feels his soften before he shakes her off. *Come on, honey, let's just dish on Maude.*

On the back cover, a photograph of Maude, now in her mid-forties like the two of them. She's leaning forward on a white sofa wearing a black silk shift.

Her white-blonde hair is only a few inches long and her eyes, that peculiar aqueous green, look both knowing and slightly shopworn.

She's still madly gorgeous, Z says.

She's a thing, all right, Childress says.

She used to be a total slob and came in with wet paint all over her clothes at all hours of the day. Why would she ever buy a white sofa?

Childress takes the book away from her and looks more closely at the photo. *It's her penthouse on the Upper East Side. I guarantee there are white carpets and a view you would die for.*

And someone running around after her cleaning up paint spills?

I told you: she's a thing, a T-H-A-N-G. Who says she's happy? I wouldn't want to be her.

The shop bell rings and the brittle-boned saleswoman who had been ignoring them makes a move as if to stand. The spell breaks when a few tourists come in.

Z would bet she and Childress will never be friends again and they never really were, but they had marked time together.

After Childress leaves, Z buys the book. At least Z knew not to share her experience of Yellow with Maude. And maybe she gave Maude the faeries, but they weren't really hers to have. Maude made something of them, and Z wasn't ready for anything then. Or now, for that matter.

The thin woman with the aged hands, wearing an elegant cashmere sweater set, bends to write out her receipt with a flourish as if they are in some bygone era. *There's no need to succeed*, that's what Clem had said to her the last time she'd seen him.

The woman hands her the book in brown paper. She smiles, and Z watches how every wrinkle in her face creases together like a moving tactile sculpture.

Your time is coming, dear, the woman says. Z startles, but she smiles back. Clem also said that other strange phrase: *This moment is the exit without the sign.*

The shop bell rings as Z leaves.

oOo

Z was at an artist residency in Virginia when the TV show came on. She was forty-eight but still small and unassuming, enough so that she looked a decade younger. Her small shows, installations, and the grants she applied for kept her moving from state to state six months out of the year. She often worked as an artist-in-the-schools, going to schoolrooms and auditoriums to talk about art, and to get kids motivated with projects across the country. Something she'd wanted when she was a child. To be with the visiting artist, not the teachers.

But it made her an itinerant worker, of sorts, hooking up with the same commitment-phobic lovers as herself—sometimes men, sometimes women—or sometimes falling into dire friendships with one of the teachers: younger straight women who found Z's small brown mouse guise attractive. She longed for them too; the friendships were fraught with endless teasing, and often came to nothing.

She didn't try too hard for the artsy look anymore. Just her black silver studded belt, her cropped sleek head. The dark laced boots. She only had to be quiet, to reflect what the person across from her, or under her, or on top of her, wanted her to be. But all of these contortions had become less so. Who was she trying to please? More and more she kept to herself.

The residents this time were a mixed bag and mostly younger than her: two ceramicists, a composer, a textile artist, a poet, and even a dancer. Plus, an almost feline-looking, T-shirted Indian-American photographer, Aakash. She estimated that they were the closest in age; he had graying hair and, from what she overheard, a different and more lucrative career before photography. His taut chest appeared to carry messages to them every night at dinner. The first were logos from his past: *Choate, Stanford, MIT, EarthLink.* She overheard him talking at the long dinner table to others about his wild and downward spiral from wealthy techie to hand-to-mouth photographer.

Gradually, his T-shirt messages became more subtle. *Freedom*, one T-shirt said. She was too far away to see if the artist sitting next to him had gotten him to talk about the shirt. The next night, when he turned around, carrying a casserole dish back to the communal kitchen, she read *Respect* and what looked like its Sanskrit twin beneath.

The first Friday night, when the cook was off, she joined those who had stayed the weekend. They shared food and had decided to binge-watch *Unsolved Mysteries* on the one TV in the communal house at the bottom of the winding tree-lined path. Aakash passed around a joint, and she could not stop watching his graceful hands. Dark with tapered fingers, yet strong and sure. She had yet to talk to him; she couldn't ignore the only other gay woman, Claudia, the textile artist, who had sat next to her and had been eyeing Z all week.

Aakash had become the group's center, the unacknowledged leader, though watching *Unsolved Mysteries* had been the young-thirties poet, Geoff's, idea. Poets like Geoff, especially white male poets, seemed the most insecure, wanting to appear cynical and trendy; they name-dropped right and left.

Z found herself wedged on the secondhand sofa between Claudia's bountiful hips and Aakash's trim frame. Geoff and Justine, the composer, were on a loveseat next to them. Justine's amber eyes offset her dark skin; she raised eyebrows and tilted her head when Geoff spoke. Z frequently sat next to Justine; she was only twenty-three but had both a solid practicality and a tenderness that Z admired. Z liked how she was entirely open to Geoff—her deep, soothing voice and the amber eyes a rich composition in themselves. Z admired how she had no judgment of Geoff.

As they watched the show, the weed began to hit her in a way she feared, or maybe it was the fear these shows induced that excited her nerves. The murderers were still at large. Of course, that was the point. So the episodes, spliced with stills from crime scenes, were often grainy and incomplete. Black-and-white photographs with tar pools of blood next to prone feet in ripped nylons flashed on the screen and prickled in Z's chest. The scenes were designed to do this, she knew: to hold your throat just to let it go again. But that choking feeling of the unresolved—Clem's death, even her mother's—threatened to take her under. The mood the show invoked reminded her of the deep unwilled part of herself that had stopped speaking. They were on their third episode, and some watched, and some talked, and Z began to feel peculiarly alienated from everyone as she sat on the dark sofa. In this episode, a girl, maybe fourteen, had been murdered during the late summer of 1972 in Acworth, Georgia. Her dark hair was parted in the middle, her prominent forehead in the school photo made her look thoughtful and moody. Z, of course, had been eleven that year. *The summer before Yellow* was the thought that drifted through her mind.

Aakash's hand came to rest near her left knee. He was leaning a little bit across Z's lap to talk to Justine, and for a moment, the hand began to look like a beautiful dark scroll. She wanted to cut a silhouette of it and to put it in one of the many shadow boxes she had been composing—shadow boxes of individual silhouettes that would form some larger whole that she couldn't yet visualize. But she had lost track of how the girl had been killed. Z turned to Claudia, whose eyes lit when Z said, *How'd she die?*

Strangled, Claudia said with an apologetic shrug. *He strangled all of them.*

An old local news report came on, the footage oversaturated with color, and a reporter held a bulbous black mic to the face of a young pregnant mother asking her what she'd seen.

We thought it was a father and his daughter, the mother said. *They were standing right out there near the shore, splashing each other and stuff. I never did see them leave.*

Z's heart began to throb; her jaw clenched. It was inevitable that the face that appeared on the TV, an artist's sketch made from the witnesses' descriptions, was the man in aviator sunglasses at Lake Pontchartrain. She hadn't remembered the receding hairline; she never knew the color of his eyes. *Green*, the narrator said.

On the TV, the pregnant woman said that she had seen him take Jennifer out of the lake water on his shoulders. She said that Jennifer's family was nearby—a large group, more than seven kids, having a cookout. That no one saw her leave the area was the tragic mystery, a detective intoned. The slow zoom onto Jennifer's school photo—her trusting, wise forehead—was almost more than Z could bear.

Z's entrenchment back into some hollow part of herself had begun. The show was manipulating her, she knew, just as this man had. Better to keep still. His name was Leonard Holiday, and he'd been a lieutenant in Vietnam. Z could feel the memory sharpen in her body: she could feel her own teeth, jagged under her tongue, and all the joints in her spine had begun to stiffen.

They said he had been involved in several raids on villages in Vietnam; they said he'd been present in two different incidents of friendly fire. They showed pictures of him with other soldiers against a tropical landscape, some slouching against a Jeep, some grinning with fingers raised in peace signs. This man, Holiday, was crouched on one knee with his rifle, his lips one flat line. They interviewed one of the vets, a fellow soldier, his face now wizened, his dark hair pebbled with gray, who said Leonard had a mean set to him.

Just the kind they wanted there. He was responsible for those friendly fires, no doubt in my mind. If the war hadn't ended, they would've discharged him anyway. The camera held to the old vet's face a few beats too long, and Z did not have to hear where they discovered Jennifer, or to see some age progression of how Holiday's particular physical housing had weathered.

She hunched into herself, tears strafed her face, and her body was rocking when she looked up to see Justine crouching at her feet holding her hands and to smell Aakash's spicy scent, his dark eyes finding hers.

Come on, Z, let's get out of here, Justine said. And then it was the three of them, these kind people on either side of her. Supporting her at first. She saw the strange flashing eyes of the group as they left. Claudia wanted to go with them, and Aakash put a hand out, touching her shoulder and saying they had it. It was all okay.

Just let it, girl. Just let it, Justine said to Z, her arms embracing Z's trembling shoulders. And down the trail through the dark woods, Z began to wail—it wasn't her, or it was. It came from the captured place, it came from the lake water, and Jennifer. Jennifer's open wonder snuffed out.

They all sat among a rough circle of stones in a clearing.

Get closer, Aakash said, and they held hands loosely. The sound of Z's pain now had Clem's loss in it, and her mother's.

When the sobs began to break, like waves slowly rolling back, she heard Aakash say, *You go to the top of her head, and I'll go to her back, okay?* Sitting cross-legged in front of her, Justine cradled Z's bent head, rubbing her temples. Z felt Aakash's strong hands moving along her backbone, finding the painful knots there.

Stray words came from them now and then, exchanged. Like a music.

Holiday's face came to mind, and then Yellow, the way she had thrown the plums into their enveloping center.

That man's still alive, Z heard herself say.

Justine said, *Whatever he did to her, or to you . . . ?* It was a question.

Z nodded.

Whatever he did, it's not you anymore, Justine said.

Z felt Aakash's hands on her back, light, like a filigree of movement, like Yellow curling, advancing.

That man's still alive, Z said, but she didn't sound as sure now.

Is he? Aakash said. *Is he really, Z?* She didn't know what he meant, and then something deep in her did, but it was hard to hold on to.

The three of them went quiet, then Z looked up to see how they surrounded her. Behind them, a flat magnificent moon. Justine's lips smiled and all three of them put their foreheads together in complete soundlessness.

A room opened where she heard their breathing. She remembered the three graces at the Met: Aglaia, Euphrosyne, and Thalia, their arms draped around each other's shoulders. Then, the room opened to be so spacious that she realized they'd vanquished the room, and they'd vanquished the story, the unsolved mystery. Yellow's consciousness had taken her in completely that night at twelve and now here, so many years later, she felt her mind go to that one big place like a large crystal palace unfolding.

oOo

Mission Control: *When the two Skylab astronauts popped the hinge, flying into space, to the complete ends of their tethers, we experienced LOS.*

Interviewer: *That would be Loss of Signal, correct?*

Mission Control: *Correct. We didn't know what was going on. It was about an hour plus. And then, we got amps . . . We saw some draw from the solar shield. Conrad came back on, said real upbeat, as I remember: 'Well, we got her done.'*

Interviewer: *Astronaut K. never mentioned that hour plus without communications.*

Mission Control: *Right. Never heard either of them talk about it again. But he told me he lost sight of Conrad during that time.*

Interviewer: *How's that possible?*

Mission Control: *You tell me.*

oOo

Holiday was so human that he was a burning seed in everyone.

No, his mother had loathed him.

No, she tossed him out of bed when his brother came.

No, she'd cut him out, cut the thread that bound them, saying, *Get out. Get out now.*

No, the priest touched him there.

No, the neighbor boys said those things about him, his mouth gear. Yelling through the fence at all hours of the day.

No, he had not done that, he convinced himself.

No, he tried dating women, but soon the edges of their mouths curled up in derision, and then he walked to the mailbox wearing his knee-high socks and slippers to collect the flat ambiguous packages.

Then the packages weren't needed because there was the Internet.

He quit the job at school because he wanted to smash the little girls' eyes.

He looked for girls that no one noticed. The ones their families had ignored.

He looked for girls that wanted to run but could not.

He looked at their necks. The luster there.

Fire and breath. Fire and breath.

He went to the next town and the next.

This apartment he filled with plants, tropical like in Nam.

All of them breathing at once.

This one bare as a bulb.

He worked security at night.

He was isolated and unresolved.

He roamed the dark parking garage looking in the messy cars, seeing things he wanted to see.

His mother was brutal.

He'd seen the singeing fire of Jesus walking towards him across the lake. A warning.

A stop.

He woke in the middle of the night because of the goblins yanking at his shorts, yanking at his cock, yanking.

There were the women and children fleeing from the burning, there were the girls fleeing, there was pounding, and that face kept looking, turning with her bright light that he was bound to put out.

Bound to.

Yes.

oOo

Each person could be said to have their wound. Did they retract and calcify around it? Did they try to keep it hidden? How does the body manifest the wound?

Without knowing how or why, wounds became the contents of her shadow boxes. Some, Z realized, could be small as matchboxes, some were larger—and formed the glass hexagonal boxes that radiated from the still empty center.

She didn't yet feel neutral about wounds.

She didn't yet feel that Holiday's wounds were worthy of the giant cell of images she was creating.

oOo

Aakash sat across from her at dinner one night when she finally decided to ask him. She, Justine, and Aakash usually headed for the end of the table to sit together, though the other residents always peered down along the pine tabletop looking Aakash's way for something: confirmation, direction?

She watched as he talked to Claudia. His index finger lightly grazed one of her knuckles, and she saw how Claudia's forehead relaxed, her lips rising to a smile. No doubt he was asking her, in all seriousness: *How is your work going?* Z's not sure how he did it, but his questions and his calm steadied each person.

The beauty of his hands wanted their way into her work though she wasn't sure why. After dessert, finally, when both Claudia and Justine stood holding goblets of wine near the screen door, she used his gesture, a light touch across the table.

He smiled at Z, his eyes holding hers, *Oh, gladly*—he answered after she asked. *I would like to be a participant in your art. But you should see all sides*, and he turned over his left hand.

On his wrist, the scar was crooked but two to three inches in length. The dark skin paler where the scar was.

If I'd just had the courage to do both, he said, cocking one dark eyebrow.

Z's eyes softened in his.

Sympathy not needed, he said. *We all have our wounds. And for me, it was the ultimate wake-up call.*

She'd never seen it. The scroll of his elegant hands had hypnotized her not to see what was plainly underneath. Wounds, exactly what her project was about.

That is how my career in Silicon Valley bottomed out, he said. *In a bathtub of my own blood. But it has a much happier ending. As you can see.* He opened his palms to her.

At her studio the next day, Z photographed Aakash's hand: scrolled and unscrolled. Then, the underside of his left wrist. It resembled nothing less than what it was: his stitched-together survival.

oOo

On July 14, 1930, Einstein welcomed Rabindranath Tagore, Indian poet, philosopher, and Nobel Laureate, into his home in Berlin for a series of discussions on science and humanity.

For Einstein, truth was at issue, and truth involved the objective reality or permanence of all things. A table, for instance, that exists independent of the human mind. Einstein said, *We attribute to Truth a super-human objectivity; it is indispensable for us, this reality which is independent of our existence and our experience and our mind—though we cannot say what it means.*

And Tagore answered: *Science has proved that the table as a solid object is an appearance, and therefore, that which the human mind perceives as a table would not exist if that mind were naught. At the same time, it must be admitted that the fact that the ultimate physical reality is nothing but a multitude of separate revolving centers of electric force, also belongs to the human mind.*

A table, therefore, could be a door.

In Tagore's book of translated prose poems, a restless traveler knocks *at every alien door to come to his own, and one has to wander through all the outer worlds to reach the innermost shrine at the end.*

The traveler says: *My eyes strayed far and wide before I shut them and said, 'Here art thou!' The question and the cry, 'Oh, where?' melt into tears of a thousand streams and deluge the world with the flood of the assurance: 'I am!'*

oOo

Z had two weeks left at the artist's residency. But only a few days with Justine and Aakash. Their residencies were complete in three days—on Monday. New artists would cycle in, and the triad they had formed would be no longer. A lesson she had to keep learning: finding and losing people she met, people who had found their way into her heart but who would pass through and disappear, eventually.

On tonight's studio walk, each of the artists opened their studios to share what they had accomplished during their time there. No surprise that she, Aakash, and Justine walked in a group, keeping themselves slightly apart.

At her cabin, Justine played her compositions: a child's music box layered with sounds of water, a heartbeat, then Justine herself on a cello. The musical patterns echoed and repeated with a solemn throb. Z had never heard anything so earthly and so unearthly. Of course, Justine radiated this genius, so like the candle's glow behind her as she leaned into her cello.

At Z's loft, the other residents gazed at the tight cluster of shadow boxes extending from ceiling to floor: some of the hexagonal boxes that formed the whole were over two feet high, some like small clouds. But not all the boxes were filled. The one at center most obviously blank.

The story's incomplete, she explained. *The composition is still unresolved.*

As they stood in front of her assemblage, what she had titled *Boxed: Shadow Selves*, the other artists in the group talked about it the way Z would have a decade ago. They talked about disjunction and the refraction of glass. Geoff compared the boxes to a John Ashbery poem. He quoted a few abstract lines in an abstract way, with his chin raised.

The many black silhouettes were broken by the one grayish photograph of the inside of Aakash's wrist in the lower left quadrant. The lone photograph had thrown her concept into question. Was she going to turn all the boxes into photographs? And what would be at the center of the large cell? She didn't know yet.

I am not ashamed of it, Aakash had told her when she took the photo. But unless he claimed his own image, Z would not speak of it. Aakash only quietly smiled, listening to her and the others, then saying, unexpectedly: *So magnificent.* He did not share what he was working on. *Still in transitu*, he said. Everyone nodded without comprehension.

At the end of the studio tour, near the hexagonal blooms of a mountain laurel, the three of them stood together. They'd made no plans for the weekend, and so it was time to say their goodbyes. It wouldn't kill her to lose Aakash and Justine too, Z knew. She'd done it before. Sometimes she'd stayed in touch with other artists that she'd connected with, and sometimes their communications eventually dwindled to nothing. It was Aakash who spoke first.

I'd like to take a trip with you two. At the lake, tomorrow night.

A trip? Justine asked. *And, by the way, I'm not a swimmer.* Her throaty laugh.

I've never liked water either, but I guess that goes without saying, Z said, but lightly.

Ever had mushrooms? Aakash asked. She and Justine looked at each other, shaking their heads, and he smiled. *I think you'll like the water*, he said, breaking from the mountain laurel a fistful of the whitish flowers—petals lined with cherry-red stitches.

He handed them each a small bunch. *These, you'll want in water too*, he said, the smile dancing into his eyes.

oOo

Illusion is in the eye of the observer, so the Copenhagen interpretation proves. You could call the study's physicists, Niels Bohr and Werner Heisenberg, Einstein's rivals. The pair who collapsed Einstein's argument for an objective reality. But, in fact, despite their heated debates at conferences, they all wrote long letters to each other. Were colleagues, perhaps friends even? They'd all won Nobel Prizes for their discoveries; they had all lived through World War II.

Some say it was Bohr and Heisenberg who discovered the real magic. Observed, reality acts just as we want it to—as particle, matter—concrete and subject to our expectations. Unobserved, photons become waves, become probabilities—events rather than objects. Pure possibility. The unexpected. The ground taken away.

Heisenberg went on to formulate the uncertainty principle. *There is no essential limit to what we can know about a quantum system. The more precisely one knows a particle's position, the less one can know about its momentum and the opposite is also true.*

Truth becomes simple: if you observe and measure, try to pin it down, the world may just fulfill your expectations of what you want it to be. Minus the witness, variety occurs and, maybe, impossibilities.

oOo

Z chews on the mushrooms from a small earthen plate that Aakash extends to her. The three of them are gathered on the wooden dock near the lake. Justine's just-releasing smile, then they clasp their hands together after eating the fungi—laughing aloud at the word. They talk lightly as the atmosphere begins to move her. Z cannot deny the erotics of the sun, the erotics of its descent, the play of its musculature over lake water.

The erotics of earth in her mouth. *Earthenware*, Z thinks, her laugh floating.

Just one tip: take it or leave it. Ask the mushroom, and it will give you your answer, Aakash says.

Dimensions of clouds take shape, Z thinks.

Dimensions of color, Aakash says. Had she said that aloud? She must have.

And sound, says Justine.

The gospel of their erotics—the sky over them like an ocean, both disparate and whole. Then their slow melting into the dock like a human star unfolding from above. Collapsed, their bodies resemble a star of completeness. Aakash says he feels as though he can rise above them to look down. *It's happened to me before*, he says.

Really? Z asks, but he doesn't answer.

Justine hears the intricacies of sound. Her composer's ear tuned to water licking the shore, insects beginning an insistent thrush, both orchestral and plain.

Patterns begin: geometrics flickering over the lake. They undress, laugh together, and float on paddleboards touching the lake's surface.

At first, each of them still holds their fear privately, like a rosebud: Z's violent initiation into sex, Aakash's whorled and lonely near-death, Justine's loss of everything she ever loved.

Justine's truth: what they do not know yet.

Gently rocking on lake water, Z hears each of them begin the honest talk of what has wounded them. Grace bends and plays among them.

Around the lake, Justine hears the trees breathing.

Their roots, she says, a stitch in her voice, *are a network of mouths.*

Aakash says that the Earth's chakras are like our own: *Feel how it vibrates from the bottom to the top?*

Z watches the geometric Aakash sitting cross-legged on his board: his body young, then old, then young again, flexing in frames that cohere then dissolve like a kaleidoscope.

He touches each chakra, and they follow.

From the root, the muladhara, he says, *to the sacral,* svadhisthana, *to the solar plexus,* manipura, *to the heart,* anahata, *to the throat,* vishuddha, *to the third eye, your* ajna. *Then out through the crown,* sahasrara. In Z's eyes, he has become older than the planet. In Justine's, he vibrates from his spine.

Yet Justine's ear still attunes to the trees: their lush quaking over water. Their many voices—a convergence. A deep, buried network that elucidates the ills of the world, including the violent split that has always made her other, has made all dark people other. This she tries to put into words.

It's hard to explain, she says, floating a little away from them, her profile touched by water droplets that glisten like small rainbows across her dark skin.

Being Black means we walk in the world like our pain is somehow less. But we know the truth . . . She floats silently, and they wait. *The trees know too. They get it. I mean, I'm just discovering that now. Their talking.*

The trees' voices become her cradle and draw out her story. Justine describes the still form of her newborn baby freshly wet on her chest, warm with the wet, but only that.

He wasn't breathing, she says. Aakash and Z drift close. They put their arms across her shoulders as she cries. The huddled form, her son, would never be; the huddled form, their son, pulled Justine and her fiancé apart.

I was young—a teenager—sure, some would call it a mistake, but we made him. Luke was stepping up to be with me. To be with us.

What is your son's name? Z asks.

Newell, she says. Newell was their incompletion. *He happened, but then he didn't. Like nobody gets that. Like they want me to just be over it. Like I dodged a bullet or something.*

Do you still love Luke? Z asks.

Oh yes, Justine whispers. *But everyone said,* Move on, girl—you're too young. *Maybe we were, but it didn't matter. To me. We made him. Made*, she emphasizes.

What a creation you made together, Z says, drifting. Sighing at the image of their Newell.

What beauty. She says something that she's always known, but that she's never spoken aloud: *The play of Earth is about forgetting and remembering. What's important, anyway.*

She must be a couple decades older than Justine, and yet, she doesn't have any answers. In the dusk's slow insinuations, the mosquitoes swarm to her flesh. And she thinks that the raw stinging bites and the mellowing sun's feel on her torso are the same.

Then she does remember. *I only know this*, she says. Because it's what Yellow told her. *One side loves the other.*

One side loves the other, Justine repeats. Now that she's told her story, her chest finally releases that small bird inside. It has come out of her throat that she has tried hard to hold closed. Poised over her head, the small bird looks down on her. And then flies away.

Will you look at that, Justine says. She nods her head to acknowledge the bird's flight. But no one else seems to see it. *That was for me*, she mouths, her chin raised.

I think you're right, Justine. Trees know. And they remember, Z says. Was it Yellow who said that or Clem?

Justine, Aakash says, *if this is all a remembering and a forgetting, then love is all we have in it. I've gone to that. I lost my lover when I tried to kill myself. She had to save me, and who wants that? I lost my lover because I lost myself. Temporarily.* His voice holds the erotics of the earth.

Z's board bumps the edges of his, his board bumps against Justine's, and they find themselves laughing. At the word, *temporarily*, at the word, *lost.*

I see what you mean, Justine says through her laughter.

Z scratches at the bites on her legs, her belly.

If Z could predict the future, she would say that Justine will find her fiancé again, just inside a different skin.

The fireflies swarm around them in the darkening woods, and above the star of their bodies, the mind hovers. The mind's room where, once they arrive again, they will remember.

oOo

They are deep in the night when Z, Aakash, and Justine paddle back to the dock and put on their clothes.

Let's hear what the trees have been saying, Justine says.

How? Z asks.

I put my little audio bug over there in the woods, she laughs. They follow her to the recording device. They walk in as if wading through light; they are surrounded by a thicket of fireflies.

My tender feet, Aakash says. *Always my tender feet.* He crouches as the lights pixilate around him.

Z watches Justine bend to the recorder that blinks an amber light on a tree stump. Justine presses play, and they hear what they hear now: the sound of a thousand tree frogs, the incantatory mating calls of bullfrogs.

Z sits on a fallen log near to it, only to stand again, looking down. Because Yellow is there. Pulsating, quivering, across the rugged expanse.

Yellow! Her voice rises.

Where? they ask. *Who?*

Yellow. She points to where Yellow has filigreed the log. She tries to explain. Yellow, who began small, a plume like a small head when she first discovered them. This part of Yellow has overtaken the log, moves incrementally, yet swifter than she remembers.

I don't see anything, Aakash says, taking Z's hand.

I don't either, Justine says, *but I believe you. I've heard so much tonight—from the trees. And seen so much! That bird!* Her voice is dreamy. She's holding the recorder in her palm. That one bird. Her head tilts up as if looking after it. *Y'all, I'm going back to my cabin. I have all the sights and sounds I can hold right now.* In the darkness, her eyes dance as she smiles.

Do you want to come back with me? Aakash asks Z.

I do, she answers. *But not yet.*

With that, it seems that Aakash and Justine have disappeared like the fireflies. She remembers she once saw their backs, lavender against the darkness, then nothing.

The next hours are devoted to Yellow and to Clem.

oOo

Z leans forward to listen, Clem's wheat-colored hair practically alight, and Yellow is pulsing, as if breathing. Z sways to the rhythm in her head resounding with the call of tree frogs—all of it like the throbbing of one vast body.

Eliza, Clem says.

Clem, Z says. *I didn't know the grace of you when you were alive.*

But you did. Clem smiles.

I've missed you.

What is missing? I'm here all the time.

You're not.

I am, Clem insists. *Yellow expounds their presence to themself. Remember Pete's spacewalk?*

Yes, Z says. *I do.*

That's how I see spacewalk: the point where you can be in outer space by being in inner space. This is reality. When you are able to discern yourself as pure thought, the thinker that consumes all thinkers, all gods, all stories, all loves, all histories, and everybody and everything that's lived within them, from the single-celled thing we call Yellow—

Clem's thought becomes Yellow's thought, and the appearance Z knows as Clem becomes the appearance Z knows as Yellow. The voice continues.

To the most complex of primates—humankind—it all still falls within your inner space, and you are that. And everything, all of this, me talking to you, a body sitting next to you, the thought of a god, it's all in your thought. And that's Yellow . . . Yellow expounds their presence to themself . . . Remember spacewalk?

And like a circle of thought, the words go around so that they become weightless, disengaged, and do their best to approximate what is in front of Z.

oOo

After Justine and Aakash left the state of Virginia for home, Z was left with the artwork on her wall. A conundrum, with the one photograph of Aakash's inner arm and the entire large hexagon unfinished. She was also left with Yellow's words that sometimes she could remember and other times eluded her.

She wrote down all she could remember. *Presence. Thought.* And *spacewalk.* And *Yellow.* But there was so much she forgot. Or that somehow, wouldn't stick.

She began to render the silhouette of Aakash's forearm to black paper. The negative space—what was missing—became the stitches. And what of Justine's wound? Wounds could be transmuted; isn't that what the night at the lake had taught her? Through our wounds, we find grace.

So she cut from black paper the huddled form of Newell, Justine's infant son. Newell's body held in the boughs of the trees that had talked to Justine the night at the lake.

She kept to herself for the rest of the residency. She sat out on her front deck in the evening, listening to the birds wind down at dusk. She admired the mountain laurel's hexagonal shape, and she remembered the way Aakash had snapped off small bouquets and given them to her and Justine the night of the studio tour.

She went back to the photograph of Aakash's arm and cut a new silhouette. Above the empty space of those stitches the relaxed palm held blooms. The hexagons of the mountain laurel flowers with their frail red stitchery, an echo of his arm, and the blooms an echo of the larger hexagon.

But at the center, she still did not know—her wounds had transformed their last night together, but how?

oOo

In her artist's loft under the skylight, filled with that one square of stars, Z went to bed with the question: how had her wounds transformed?

That night, Clem appeared in her dream. They walked along the railroad tracks skirting New Orleans' riverfront when it began to rain, and they lay on a grassy bed below the rails. Impossible in real life. The train came from far off, dopplering its train sound. Clem shouted into the pinpricks of rain all the places he had gone when he jumped trains: *Birmingham*, *Pittsburgh*, *New York City*. He'd gone west too: *Austin*, he yelled, *Albuquerque*, *Tucson*, and *San Diego*. With every destination name, they laughed harder, throwing their arms back on the grass and letting the rain rivet their faces with pure sensation.

Pure sensation. It was the end of the dream before she knew it: Clem stood up and there was that scepter again with the pinecone at the end. She crouched to her knees as his subject. Every gesture a pantomime, every gesture part of their fun. She knelt and the pinecone came down to her face, and she saw up close the design on the bottom.

The next morning, still elated by Clem's visit, it was easy to look up the shape of the pinecone. Ah, the golden ratio. She remembered the concept from her art classes, and she cut the black paper to show the beauty of that spiral, with its nodes that could fan either way.

Clem's pinecone—how that silly affectation had been a reminder of her wound, now transformed. She had left Clem to the hurricane carrying his staff, and with one dream, Clem had made the image their joke and paramount in their last connection.

Now it was the center of her hexagon. Radiating from the cut black-paper spiral were wounds, hers and others, that she thought she couldn't contain.

oOo

Aakash called a few months after her residency ended. Out of the blue? Maybe not entirely. She had dreamed of his smooth hands the night before.

I'm coming south, he said. *I want to stop by to see the completion of your shadow boxes.*

How did you know I finished them? Z said. *They're up in a space in town.*

I just know you, Z, Aakash had said on the call. *Of course you finished it. Of course, it is already loved.*

She didn't say it covered an entire brick wall in a whiskey bar. Childress had emailed her after she'd arrived home from the residency, asking if she had any new work. And then, when she sent him some digital images, he asked her if he could give it a trial run on the brick wall of the bar, adjacent to the gallery.

It's gorgeous. If no one buys it, I will. A permanent Z installation, let's say.

Who would say no? Once assembled on the wall—the rough red bricks behind each glass hexagon looking like the very ground of being—Childress said: *I'm attached. I mean, I'm really, really attached. You're such a witchy beast to attempt something so grand. Fuck if it hasn't succeeded.*

Of course, she was so happy to see Aakash. He pulled up in front of the café across the street in an orange Karmann Ghia, packed full, it seemed, with everything he owned.

You better park your car in our courtyard if you want to keep any of that, she said, laughing as they hugged. She showed him all her New Orleans haunts. He liked especially the shadow of the Christ thrown on the back wall of St. Louis Cathedral.

They stood on the flagstones of Pirate's Alley looking at the enlarged Christ, holding out his arms. The jambalaya of smells was one of the things she treasured most about New Orleans: the star jasmine, the dark earth and moss greens, the gritty flagstones slicked with water, even the faint tincture of the urine of the impoverished.

What a metaphor of belief, he said. *All of us, every one, throwing shadows against the wall. Jesus is just the big one.*

Hmmm, good point. Z thought of her years of attending Mass—at least her love for beauty and grandeur were satisfied there. *This courtyard used to be even better,* Z said. *But the hurricane took down the great oaks. Well, not really better. Just different.*

They traipsed through the Quarter to the whiskey bar, taking in the energetic live music and street poets, and finally each stood in front of *Boxed: Shadow Selves* with a snifter of some specially aged concoction with a trendy name that Z would never remember.

Ah, I see that my forearm did make the cut. He looked into her eyes, and they both laughed at his pun. *And you have used black paper after all. Good choice. Yes.* He raised an eyebrow, taking in the flowers.

And Newell, Aakash said in a low whisper. His lips pressed together, and she watched his eyes tracing the skeletal branches that held the infant. He stroked the little goatee that he had grown. She liked how a few of the gray hairs sprung from the darker hair like silver threads.

You are very talented, Z. And to include at the center the third eye. That is the very genius of it.

She stood silent. The third eye? You mean the golden ratio? she wanted to ask, but Z did not say this aloud. She waited, trying to puzzle out why he thought the pinecone was a third eye.

But she had no idea. Only later, as their bodies wound together in a way she'd never experienced and only later, as the silk of their skins rubbed almost through each other, did she say in the fragrant dark, their heads tilted together, did she say: *Why did you say there is a third eye at the center of the shadow boxes? It's the bottom of the pinecone scepter that my brother carried around. I never knew why.*

Your brother did. All over the world, the pineal gland right here between your eyebrows—Aakash touched the center of her forehead—*has been symbolized by the pinecone . . . Hindus believe it represents your third eye.*

Of course, Clem always knew more than she did. Of course, he had led her to just this point, where this beautiful man held a finger to her forehead.

oOo

They defined each other as friends, and yet the elasticity of their relationship grew to hold all parts of each other. Part of the freedom they showed each other was to recognize what wasn't changeable or negotiable: Z's need for privacy, Aakash's need to socialize. They would never own each other nor try to modify the other's behavior to fill something in themselves. So many other habits that they broke or didn't break.

Aakash's parents still wanted him to marry an Indian bride. At the beginning of every month, the matchmaker they had hired would send him two to three profiles of eligible women. He felt a duty to appease his parents. A duty, he explained, because of his attempted suicide and the loss of his fiancée Anjali. The outcome: Aakash would spend two to three evenings a month on first dates.

Z did not ask how the dates went. Perhaps he really was still looking. When a woman walked by her in yoga pants in the coffee shop, and her eyes were pulled to lustful fantasies, maybe she was still looking too. Though inside, Z knew the difference. She felt eternally pulled to Aakash.

Eventually, Aakash told his parents to save their money. He was no longer following up these profiles and said he was very happy on his own.

Z was not a secret to them; Aakash introduced her to his parents as his friend. In her old apartment on Barracks and Decatur, they had become roommates with private rooms and bathrooms and a shared living room and kitchen. Z knew Aakash's entire family. In her unassuming way, and possibly because she referred to former girlfriends, Z had escaped their notice. *I think they think of me as the gay best friend without the comic relief,* Z said once.

Or the wild fashion sense, Aakash added.

Do I have a fashion sense? Z asked. Aakash shrugged.

She was spared his parents' evaluation as he intended, and Z's family accepted Aakash as her friend and roommate.

Her father died suddenly, a heart attack in the new Barcalounger at Frank's house. Z asked Aakash not to attend the funeral with her. Cheryl asked what *art project* Z was working on as they held paper plates at Janice's house after the service.

All eyes turned to Z but puzzled and with consternation. *Nothing really*, Z said. The awkward group let out a sigh. Talking about anything besides the Saints and home mortgages excited their nerves.

If Aakash and Z were going to come together, they would come together as Yellow did. The math was simple. *For Yellow: 1 + 1 = 1*, Z said.

That we are separate at all is a myth, Aakash said. In this way, Aakash sometimes spoke the way Clem had. Reminded her of what she had forgotten.

The pull to Aakash never ceased. If at first it was his hands that Z had adored, then there were new luxuries: the beauty of his profile, his lean and erect cock, the way he whispered into her ear, taunting her, pleasuring her, giving to her.

When she came, he wanted her to come more; when he came, she felt the vibrations in her own pelvis, even after their bodies had parted. Even lying separately, panting, Z felt the rippling of his pleasure.

They often traveled on their own. Aakash to many spiritual gatherings, Z to her art residencies at schools in different states. There had been no person more tender to her than Aakash.

This is bound to go wrong, Aakash said one day as they reclined together watching an old black-and-white movie, and Z was surprised.

Why do you say that? It was Z who frequently thought this—that one day the gravitational pull would simply stop. But their one day, their one moment—if tended to—felt everlasting. Aakash slipped a hand under her shirt and guided her hand to his cock.

Because we will get old, he said.

I guess we'll have to adapt, she replied, and the movie, the crumpled socks stuffed into the couch, the hilarity of Mardi Gras proceeding outside in the streets without them, faded into oblivion in the all-encompassing motion of their bodies merging again and again.

She knew more now about Yellow. The slime mold she and Clem had discovered as children has 720 sexes, but what exactly does that mean in a one-celled organism? From what Z could tell, even by 1975, not long after Yellow had escaped, scientists determined that 720 DNA sequences would mean at least 360 ways of finding each other.

Different mating behaviors, Z often thought. In other words, like Yellow, when she and Aakash loved each other, their sex was endlessly different and new. Was, essentially, in the moment and far from routine.

oOo

The dynamics of quantum mechanics were what Einstein could never resolve. He identified the photon, discrete packets of energy, or quanta, but some say it was his moral quality that set him on the lonely path as an unexpected opponent of quantum theory.

In his later years, he no longer gave lectures, wrote long letters to colleagues, and stuck close to the Princeton campus, trying to work out his unified field theory, trying to find the equation.

After an aortic aneurysm, Einstein refused extreme measures, preferring to die when he wanted to, *elegantly.* On his deathbed, it was as if he were on a groundless ground.

In the unified field theory, his lifelong compulsion to *uncover the invisible forces in the universe* finally did take into account quantum mechanics, and yet, the theory couldn't incorporate our primary anchor: gravity.

oOo

You have a beautiful back, Jilly once said, as Z reached for a tangled T-shirt at the end of the bed. It was early in the relationship, and Z still cared for Jilly's doe eyes and what Jilly saw there. When they huddled close together, Z's palm on Jilly's ample breast, Z said, *What makes it beautiful?*

The way I can see every node of your spine and those places under your shoulder blades.

You mean, my scapula? Z corrected, and Jilly's eyes darted away. She was sorry for that now. All her judgments. All her failures to love well.

We cannot see our own backs. In the same way that the sun cannot see itself. In the same way we cannot see ourselves in the eyes of the beloved.

When Z's art met its public, she often found that it lost its art, at least for her. Her art shape-shifted in the eyes of who was looking and that buoyant gasp of air that she felt for it—its absolute wholeness and richness, its erotics—somehow deflated.

It's the mistake of attachment, you know, that duality, Aakash said—*to hold something up as stellar, as better, even to suspect it is whole and complete without its dark side. You're setting yourself up.*

Don't we all? For love and for art? Z asked.

And for life? Aakash said. *For the sun, there is no opposite, no duality.* He was holding her, saying these words, his warm chest against her warm back. Things were easy with Aakash. He admired her art; she admired his.

What about the moon? She thought of Pete—she thought of Pete saying it was the best movie ever. That moon landing. She thought of the fact that we only see the same side of the moon.

After she told Aakash about Pete Conrad, they looked him up. On YouTube they heard his laugh—how many miles did that laugh travel—from moon to Earth? *The Pete Conrad laugh*, as they said in Mission Control.

What does the sun know of the moon? Aakash said.

He was the sun for her or so Z felt. When he was joyful, he radiated comfort. He radiated peace. Rarely was he anything but sun.

Just as Z had told Aakash about Yellow, Aakash had told her about his near-death experience when he had tried to kill himself. *Now that I know what death is really like, fear is extinguished. In the face of death, I will not shrink*, he said. Z thought of the moon's implacable face always turned to us.

All sun, all the time, Aakash would say. *Because, why not?* Z remembered how she first knew him by the phrases on his T-shirt. *Freedom, respect.* Those two qualities carried them both through the hard times.

oOo

Of space, Pete knew possibility. On September 13, 1966, from the port side of Gemini 11, during an unexpected eleven minutes when the capsule lost contact with Earth, he saw an unidentified flying object. Understood then, as he watched the spiraling, flexing shape—thousands of feet in size—what he needed to know.

Pete said in his debriefing that he and crewman Richard Gordon saw the object from the small capsule's narrow forward view window as it flew out in front of them. They discussed it, decided to take pictures, and he took four, stopping to advance the film with each photo. The time of his photos was 27 hours, 43 minutes Ground Elapsed Time.

After Pete took the photos, the object dropped out of sight, and Houston came back online.

> Houston, TX, Manned Spacecraft Center: *This is Gemini Control, 27 hours 52 minutes into the flight. Gemini 11 is down over South Africa on the night side of its eighteenth revolution, within range of Tananarive now. We'll standby for air ground transmission during this pass.*
>
> (27:52:26) Spacecraft: *Hello Houston, 11 here. How do you read?*
>
> HOU: *Read you loud and clear.*
>
> Spacecraft: *Okay. We had a wingman flying wing on us going into sunset here, off to my left. A large object that was tumbling at about one revolution per second and we flew . . . We had him in sight, I say fairly close to us, I don't know, it could depend on how big he is, and I guess he could have been anything from our ELSS (Extravehicular Life Support System) to something else. We took some pictures of it.*

Later, in 1968, Dick Gordon described the object looking *just like a spacecraft looks when they're flying. It was a brilliant source of light. I'd say the color was a sort of yellow-orange. It looked just the way the sun reflects off most metals up there. It had to be made of something like a metallic material to reflect light the way it was doing. There was nothing that we could distinguish as having shape. We thought the object was tumbling because it would flash. You know, the reflected light from it would be flashing.*

The day after the sighting, the North American Aerospace Defense Command issued their report to follow up NASA's explanation that the astronauts had seen a Russian satellite, the Proton 3, or its spent boosters:

> *We have a report on the object sighted by Pete Conrad over Tananarive yesterday on the eighteenth revolution. It has been identified by NORAD as the Proton 3 satellite. Since Proton 3 was more than 450 kilometers from Gemini 11, it is unlikely that any photographs would show more than a point of light.*

At his debriefing on September 21, Pete talked to James Underwood, NASA's Photo Analyst, to confirm that yes, those were the pictures he took of what he chose to call *the stranger.* Underwood, in a memo, used Pete's language when he said that if the object was 280 miles away, as stated by NORAD for the distance to the Proton, *the stranger* was *about 18 miles long.*

Ten years after the sighting, in 1976, Pete was still amused by seeing the yellow stranger, at least in a private interview. His pictures showed that the four varying-sized circles connected into one larger form was brighter than expected of a booster, and its motions from image to image fluctuated in a pattern unexpected for Russian fuselage. Pete said he saw it for about thirty seconds and was glad to get pictures.

But publicly, at the original October 1966 technical debriefing, Pete deferred to the experts:

We didn't see our own booster on orbital flight at all. We did spot the one satellite, and I thought I saw another one later, but it turned out that it was a large particle outside the spacecraft. But the satellite we picked up, boy, it was loud and clear. They told me it was 289 miles away. It must have been awfully big. I read that it was the Proton 3.

Dick Gordon said: *Oh, is that right?* What they didn't want to say was held between them.

Not much data available exists anymore on the UFO sighting by the astronauts on Gemini 11. Except from former NASA engineer and space historian

Jim Oberg, who officially identified the sighting as a Russian satellite or its booster parts.

Of space, maybe Conrad knew what the public was ready for. In the immensity of space, what's impossible? In the immensity of mind, what's probable?

oOo

In the crystal of knowing, Aakash came alive.

In the crystal unfolding above any hands of time, Aakash came alive. And Aakash was no longer steeped in the bath of his own death.

Instead, he floated above the scene that no longer held him: he saw the weight of his body, glistening in the bath—plumes of red floating—like bright ribbons that were his anchors and his attachments.

How curious, Aakash thought, floating above the Aakash that had sunk to that.

I am that? Aakash questioned. Without pause, he was in Anjali's thoughts: N*o, no, no, no*, and her banging at the door—her heart in her throat. Oh, he felt her heart beating from the inside, and then her entire life force bursting through the door, screaming his name.

Her beautiful, long black hair drenched in the water and pulling the Aakash body—that thing—to the surface.

He had left that body, wanted to leave that thinginess that kept tugging him to what he couldn't do, couldn't be, hadn't yet become. How he had tried to get to the top as his parents wanted, but something in him would drag him back to the nub of his own mirrors—what he couldn't do, couldn't be, hadn't yet become—

His company, finally, taken from him, the company he'd dreamed of, the company that had become him, had become his very arrogance, his grasping. The new awareness looked around: it was the marble bath, it was the faucets he'd chosen, it was the *Architectural Digest* Aakash. It was who he'd become—this thinginess—and it was also the narcissus opening next to the bath—

Its fragrance what he had missed—as of flesh, as of the body becoming and ceasing to be—

But now the crystal of his life opened again, and there was no remorse to leave the scene where Anjali begged on the phone for someone to come: *Come right away!* she screamed.

There was no remorse to be floating—weightless outside of his body where, with one thought, he was with his parents, resided near them as they watched TV together, blue light passing over their faces, the cluck under his mother's tongue, the deep sigh in his father's resignation—such beauty in the daily. Even the beauty of their bodies turning away from each other, huddling to their own fierce needs—

He saw his sister in Baltimore, caring for her four-year-old son—the two of them laughing together as she read aloud from a book—the small bedside lava lamp pulsing in time with their blood—ah, appearances!

His eyes opened once, and then his eyes opened again. The crystal of his life sent him across the planet where all the thoughts of the living became the crystal itself. Every thought and entanglement of his former life with others became clear to him:

The day his parents left him at boarding school—the feeling of being emptied, lost—and his mother's hasty kiss on his head—betraying nothing. He had sunk further into himself, thinking they didn't want him anymore. But now, he saw how she had willed herself not to clasp him too tightly. *Let Aakash go*, her thoughts said. *Oh, I see*, he realized. She was letting me go for my own good.

The crystal showed him the weak moments and the strong—where he had discounted others, where others had discounted him, yet everyone held blameless in the crystal's eye.

He was again near the bath where the paramedics bent to his wet seal-like body, draining of color—he watched as Anjali stepped away and slumped against the wall and to the floor, where she erected her own little barricade, looking at what had become of Aakash.

If a crystal unfolds, what is at its center?

He was. And at that moment that is all moments, among beings of light and the love that pulsed and held him within—it was like nothing he'd felt before.

The light that couldn't be anything other than the source of—what? Words failed, thoughts failed—and were no longer needed.

The crystal unfolded and he recognized Durga, remembered going into the Hindu temple with his aunt and uncle when he stayed with them in Mumbai as a teenager.

His uncle, flicking Aakash's back saying, *Stand up straight*. Now, Aakash knew everything that bore down on his uncle to have said it. He saw again the goddess with seven arms, fighting with myriad weapons, on the back of a tiger. Such fierce fighting. To destroy everything—to bring it all down to begin anew.

Is that what Aakash had done? Destroyed everything?

Durga's face was his mother's face, was his father's face, became, he saw, America's face, and was his own.

In the crystal of knowing, there were no faces, there were no bodies, yet every presence was known to him. In the crystal of knowing, there was no before and no after, there was only the throbbing simultaneity of one mysterious love.

Expect the unbelievable, a presence near to him said. *But be unattached to the outcome.*

Ahhhh, Aakash said, acquiring a knowledge inside him, acquiring all outside of him as inside of him. He asked questions of the presences gathered around him, but they no longer gave him answers, though they throbbed with a light that was all light.

Unwinding like a clock, the crystal enfolded everything within it—but they were arming him, like Durga, to go back, not to stay.

And then he felt pushed back into the meaty place where he'd always been housed, and he saw that mere moments had passed during which he had traversed space and time—that Anjali was hugging herself, trying to still the furious blood of her heart.

In the time that Aakash had vanished, Anjali had withdrawn her love from him, had replaced it with anger, and could only love herself now. Which included him too, but she did not know this yet.

She did not know that in the time that Aakash had vanished from her, Aakash had come alive.

He blinked, took a spluttering breath, and his chest heaved, coughing out more and more water. His arm throbbed where they had bandaged him. The EMTs sprung up around him, but the noises and voices blurred. Dazed, his eyes found the still petals of the narcissus, smelling of flesh, and its one yellow eye at the center. Tears poured down his face for the crystal at the center of everything, and he wept that it had closed again.

oOo

Clem told her that no one knew the existence of solar flares until Skylab. Just some stray information she now remembers, and didn't he say Pete went through the sun? Maybe it was a metaphor for knowing . . . for knowing Yellow? Sometimes Z wondered: *Did Pete actually go through the sun?*

Clem's words frequently rose in her body when she least expected it. Why didn't she say *mind*? Because Clem said to her once: *The mind is all around you, Z.*

Walking past Jackson Square one April morning, Z felt the mind as palpable. An overnight rain left the slate flagstones glistening. Mica winked beneath her booted feet and vapor lifted as if the city itself breathed the honey of possibility. Beyond the black iron fencing, azalea blooms erupted. The smell of the carriage horses, the tap of their hooves, and the gradual thickening of the air reminded Z of those days spent so close to Yellow that their escape didn't seem possible. A *translucence* is what she'd named it long ago—when the bigger mind, her mind, and the bottomless world all cohered.

The bells at St. Louis Cathedral had begun to sound and that too signaled the tolling of discovery. On St. Peter Street, Z passed the familiar paintings tied to iron railings around the square: it was the work of the UFO artist. The UFO artist always used bold primary colors in chalky paints to render her obsessive research into UFO sightings around the world. Spaceships of every possible design and aliens looking both rudimentary and light-filled were always featured on her canvases, along with blocks of lacquered typography documenting where the sighting took place and by whom. She'd gone by the woman's paintings countless times without stopping. Odessa—her signature read—with the *O* looking ocular, the *s*'s slithering along in different colors of red.

Z was on her way to the Royal Street gallery where her new wall art had been in a small show some months back. In her portfolio was a selection of custom sketches that a new client had requested. Their meeting was in twenty minutes. That Z herself had gotten her start on this same side of Jackson

Square—the Pirate's Alley side—was the kind of perfection that her current life allowed. She slowed this time going past; she wasn't sure why.

As usual, Odessa was nowhere to be seen, but the phrase in neon blue under a murky star-spattered sky caught her like a flare from space. *What Pete Saw*, the lettering read. You could tell that Pete was in a capsule, you could tell by his drop-jawed profile that he was caught unaware, you could tell that what he saw looked nothing like the green-ghostly crescents one normally associated with UFO sightings. Instead, the image was of five varying sizes of circular structures connected within something bigger. All of these were painted in yellow; just under the blue typography, two lines in white lettering: *The Yellow Stranger, Gemini 11, 1966*. The effect on her body was immediate; her breathing slowed, and she started to sweat; and then her arousal. An arousal and a recognition. She didn't know Pete had seen a UFO, a UFO that looked exactly like Yellow, magnified times a thousand.

She remembered the women with bright red braids in The House of Voodoo when she was just twelve, the summer of Yellow. There was no photograph of Odessa, but surely, she was one of the goddesses who knew, who perhaps had come from somewhere else.

Z looked around for Odessa. There was no price, but she could leave some money. She felt in her pockets and had none. She checked her iPhone. She only had ten minutes now, but the meeting would take no more than a couple hours; she'd come back.

By afternoon, the streets were thick with tourists as well as the Nawlins performance artists and panhandlers trying to make a buck.

She felt, even before she broached the intersection of St. Peter and Chartres, that Odessa might be gone, and with her, all the facts about intelligent life from other universes that she'd so lovingly made vibrant and earthly.

She was still amazed that Yellow had played a starring role in Pete's life too, had rippled and shape-shifted not as a small organism but Superdome-sized outside his spacecraft, giving him the knowing he needed to walk on the moon three years later, to laugh and feel like he was starring in the best movie ever.

Pete had co-starred all along for Clem. Did Clem know that Pete had seen Yellow?

And she was right. In Odessa's spot, nothing was left but a few stray pieces of wire along the rails. Z sat on the low wall, closed her eyes, and let the weak sun pool on her cheekbones. How many others kept the open secret of Yellow—earthly creature or space creature or really just *the* creature?

Later, entwined together on the futon bed they'd put out on her small balcony, Z told Aakash, and he laughed; he always saw numbers where she saw images. *Pete was part of the Gemini 11 crew?* Aakash asked. *Oh, that makes sense. Wasn't that your brilliant calculation: 1 + 1 = 1?*

And Gemini, the twins? What do you make of that? she asked into the fragrant dark.

Just reflections of the one. The one looking back, he said, winding her long just-graying hair around his wrist where the razor had once gone. The scar grew fainter, forgotten, then remembered.

He proposed that they look for Odessa. But Z suspected she was gone for good.

oOo

Aakash was in India when the reality of the pandemic set in. Mid-March 2020. Photographing Indian women. *It's a project of unveilings*, he said. *To get at their essence.* But perhaps, Z thought, without ever saying so, he was still looking for Anjali, the woman who had left him. Not the actual Anjali but something of her essence.

A project of unveilings, and yet, everywhere, across the world, the population had to veil, to mask in order to get well.

Z wondered whether Aakash would mask. Or whether India would.

oOo

Interviewer: *I understand that once you all landed, you had an unexpected meeting.*

Astronaut K: *That's right. It was only our third day back. They helicoptered us from the Coral Sea back to San Clemente where Richard Nixon was having a conference with Premier of Russia, Mr. Brezhnev, and so he wanted to introduce us to him.*

We were wearing these masks, supposed to wear masks to prevent us from getting infected because we were part of a medical experiment, and it's going to be another eighteen days before we are off the diet, and they stop collecting everything you put out.

We are out of the chopper and walking toward these two guys and Pete Conrad said, 'I don't like this; this is insulting to the President of the United States. Let's take these damn things off and put them in our pockets.' And so we did.

They didn't give us any diseases, and we didn't give them any diseases, and we had a conversation with these two guys, and Pete angled an invitation from Brezhnev for us to come to Russia. Sure enough, the following year, we were invited with our wives to have a tour of Russia at the peak of the Cold War. But that's another story.

oOo

Z took the causeway out of New Orleans in late June in the wreck of a car Aakash had left behind—his adorably old orange Karmann Ghia, stinking of patchouli. The COVID-19 cases had subsided somewhat, though everyone was predicting a rough winter.

Z had packed her camping gear, intending to camp as close as she could to the first lake. In the early morning fog, her lake, Lake Pontchartrain, appeared to be just a figment, swirling with all her life's blurry intentions. She knew this lake was her first marker—and that she'd come back to it again at the end of her trip. Pelicans flew close to the causeway, sometimes alone, sometimes in pairs, drifting down so close they looked like prehistoric birds.

She'd grown tired of staring at the brick wall across from her balcony. The weather-pocked wall like a southern wilderness—tufted with tendrils of ferns. She used to love her time with her morning coffee to stare into that greenery. Now, with her school residencies dried up and the galleries closed, it had become a lonely view. When she turned her chair toward the street, she could see the locals and the few tourists wandering in and out of the coffee shop on the corner of Barracks and Decatur. The baristas knew her there, and she knew them, but gradually the ones she'd known had disappeared. The young ones, students in college for the most part, had gone home to take their classes online. She worried that the older baristas had gotten sick, but who was to know? People seldom kept track of each other now, could manage only their own lives.

The Black Lives Matter protests had fired her up early in the summer, and she'd joined many of the protests in Duncan Plaza, staying late into the night, watching the barricade of police presence turn slowly human, turn back into that mélange of southern hospitality when everyone got tired and just wanted to mull in some old jazz. But there was another feeling: the old ways weren't working anymore. Too many people of color were being killed by police. What had been hidden in plain view had now become even plainer with the deaths of George Floyd and Breonna Taylor.

There was the feeling of a great screw loosening, a fragmenting with many voices.

Who was that one voice who could tell her what to do?

But Z knew there wasn't one voice that could follow all the human dramas now.

There's just one 'one,' Aakash would say. Which seemed like a good joke right about now. The fog was thick, and she could only see a few yards in front of the car. Police used to have to escort travelers across the causeway on foggy days, but now everyone traveled slowly in the well-lit right lane, marked by cones and bright lights.

Z thought the foggy view fitting to begin her trip. It had occurred to her sometime last week that she would never solve the mystery of Holiday, perhaps could never see him as part of Yellow, if she didn't go to the places where he had killed.

The thought of those other lakes brought a thickness to her throat; first she'd go to Lake Allatoona, Georgia, where they'd found Jennifer.

Maybe her life would be about recovering the unrecovered. For that's what Clem was now. Officially one of Hurricane Katrina's unrecovered. *What is there to recover?* she heard him say. The thought made her smile.

Because she could no longer see land, somewhere in the middle of the twenty-four mile causeway, Z had the sense of the expanded self. She hadn't heard from Aakash for a couple weeks, since late May. Bad cell phone service, power outages? They'd used WhatsApp, then his end had gone silent. Last she heard, he was still in Mumbai where no one he knew had gotten ill. But he wanted to travel. *I'll be fine*, he had reassured her. He felt connected there, felt energized. She knew he was right; he did feel connected. And even far away, weren't they still connected?

She'd let their communications fall off, had understood his need to go further into his art. Wasn't this the time to do it?

Z had the sense of the expanded self when the fog lifted. When she could no longer see the shore.

At one of the turnarounds, when she was still going under 15 miles an hour, Z's nerves fired. Wasn't that Clem at the wheel of an old Dodge pick-up? He wore a mask and sat next to someone she couldn't see in the passenger seat, the bed of the truck filled with a jumble of furniture. She wanted to stop, but she couldn't stop with the trail of cars behind her.

He was turning around, going back to New Orleans. The expanded self.

From above, how could Clem know?
From ground level, how could Clem know?

oOo

After that first sighting, Clem kept appearing. Roadside coming out of a Gulf station in Opelika, Alabama, near dusk. He was unmasked, loping in that way he had—one tattered Ked shoe in front of the other, hands in his pockets. He beamed at her, and she slowed the car, the knot in her throat yet to loosen. Why was he here? But as she guided her car over the pebbled entry, tapping the brakes, she saw him slide into a battered Corolla. The driver's face looked back at her, and of course, it wasn't Clem.

She kept driving, and when it was dark and she'd crossed the state line into Georgia, she stopped at the visitor's center bathroom. She wondered all the time if she was diligent enough. Did she sanitize her hands well enough? How many surfaces had she touched? Did it matter?

She overheard a mother with her young daughter in the stall next to hers.

Don't touch, the mother said, and the whimpering of the girl followed.

Don't touch, don't touch. She thought of Yellow, always touching, always trying to touch. Going to whatever expanded them. She waited for the mother and her daughter to exit. At the long line of sinks, she used an elbow to turn on the faucet and looked up to a see a gray-haired woman, wearing all black, looking back at her. Her cheekbones seemed to be more pointed, her nose looking more like her mother's, bird-like. But she'd never seen any resemblance to her father's face staring back at her, ever. She would be sixty in a matter of months, and the unknown in her was surfacing in her features. Always that question: who was she?

She headed toward the vending machines, and Clem turned around, but he was scowling, and as she got closer, he appeared to shrink until he was an aged man stroking a gray goatee, and every fiber of her being wanted to recoil. It wasn't Clem, it was Holiday, and Z reversed course, feeling the man's weak eyes riveting between her shoulders.

She remembered that dream she had as a child, that dream of being trapped in her house at the window just as her mother had been. Fear. The premonition that fear would forever reside in her and that the only path to safety was to have a man near her so that other men wouldn't stare at her in the dark.

You are that fear, Yellow had said.

She felt amused now because, in fact, that hadn't been her future. Hadn't she done it all on her own? Hadn't she gone to love's unfurling in the way Yellow had—regardless of any danger—often into the danger?

She turned around, but Holiday was no longer there. The smooth bank of lit machines—Coke, Mountain Dew, water bottles like translucent candles—seemed both alien and hyperreal. All the products behind bars. A truck idled noisily in the parking lot; people sat inside their cars like prisoners. Holiday was a figment. But one she had to go to again and again to get to the bottom of it all. *The theme of the dream is what we think we know*, she remembered Clem saying. She remembered how she discounted the things he said.

She got to Red Top Mountain State Park on the banks of Lake Allatoona in the dark and set up her tent in the glare of the Karmann Ghia's headlights.

A wooded trail beyond her car reminded her of the playthings of some former life—a life behind her suburbia. And here she was again: looking for what she'd lost.

oOo

The smell of the woods came before even the rosy light behind her eyes. When Z went to its banks, the lake was still, no waves lapping. She'd booked at the campsite where Jennifer's family had stayed those many years ago. She felt no residue of murder here any longer. Across the lake, rounded and wooded hills. Z made coffee on her camp stove and dipped her feet in the water, only slightly chilled. The sun was out, and she put on her swimsuit, pumped up her paddleboard, and floated to the middle of the lake, closing her eyes.

Smells emanated around her as if the lake water held some essential greenness—how else to describe the mucky lakebed sand, algae, and the fleet minnows escaping beneath her body in schools of blind allegiance? Or was it a knowing allegiance, to be in that working oneness?

To be alive is to have temporary use of the senses. What we take for granted. It struck her that here, minus the mask that kept the feared virus from her nostrils and her mouth, she was enjoying a freedom that everyone had barely noticed before the pandemic. COVID-19, they had learned, had the peculiar side effect of taking away the sense of smell and taste. The body's pleasures detached, useless. Z let her hand float on the surface, wanting to feel every molecule.

From nearby, she heard the calls of geese, then closing her eyes, sensed the giant *V* of their shadow passing over her torso. If only the earth could touch us closer. If only we acted like the earth were always touching us.

Jennifer, she thought. That's why she was here. She sat up on her board, paddled to a cove where she could concentrate and closed her eyes.

Jennifer's face appeared like a crystal, a diamond. Her prominent forehead could be wisdom or could be Z's love for wisdom. Her smooth skin could be the feathers of a snow owl, or it could be . . . but then Holiday's face appeared.

Z blinked her eyes open, willing the sticky nightmare of his face away. Instead, she saw the sun mulling and yellowing, thinking of what Aakash knew of the sun and what he had taught her. It cannot see itself; it is all.

And she remembered what she had taught Aakash about Yellow.

You could shred the slime mold in a blender, and it will reconstitute, will rejoin itself. Separateness is but a temporary setback. You could cut it into eight billion parts, and Yellow will reconstitute back into one cell. Wasn't that what Clem was telling her the night of her mushroom journey? As oneness becomes apparent, you see all beings emanating from one thought bigger than one person.

Holiday, though. She couldn't forgive him.

No. He was—maybe still is—an aberration. He had not been located yet. For a moment, she imagined him advancing like a chameleon on the shore, hovering amid the trees. At this lake, he had violated Jennifer, had taken her under the water, suffocating her.

He'd always sought out the lost girls, the girls no one noticed. Three had been found near lakes, were always suffocated by his large crushing thumbs over the pearls of their small throats. Z, perhaps, was the one who got away. Why? She couldn't remember why he'd left her crying in the water, his mouth agape, a blinding light in his aviator frames. Then the sickly white of his back retreating.

Tears streamed down her face for the ugliness of the human. Every fiber of her fought the idea of Holiday as part of her, as part of Yellow.

A great blue heron glided across the lake, alighted on a downed tree. *Jennifer, Jennifer, Jennifer,* she thought.

oOo

Z only managed to stay three more nights at Lake Allatoona. On either side of her, the campsites were inhabited by families, and she felt closed in. On one side of her, two boys, so like the twins when they were that age, chased each other along the red-earthed shoreline. One frequently sat in frustration by himself. Through his eyes, she could imagine seeing the pebbles next to his sneakered feet. She felt his sadness. The sadness of being different.

Maybe everyone thinks they're different. Frank had told her on the phone that Trump was his hero. She'd considered stopping to see Frank and his family on the way here, but his tirade on how masks were infringing on his rights made her feel weary. Frank's alliance made sense though.

Frank considered himself a rebel, and yet, he ate processed food advertised on his large-screen TV, collected a small arsenal in his garage, went to Mass dutifully, cuffed his children as their father had, tried to make sense of every contradiction, and never seemed to look back after Clem died.

Aakash said to her, only six months ago when they left Frank's ranch house, still lit blue like a fish tank by the television: *That is me. That is you.*

Aakash, Frank told you he thought that India is a nasty mess of shit when you talked about your trip.

Yeah, he did. They slid into the Karmann Ghia, and Aakash rolled down the window, gesturing at the small plot of woods near the collapsed cars that Frank had plans to get *fixin' on.*

I bet there are loads of great mushrooms in those woods. Some will say the psilocybin mushrooms are poisonous. Which they are, yet they are also magical to another. Right? It's just perception. That fact of perception calmed her when she felt herself going against anyone for their point of view.

On the phone, she'd said to Frank: *Sorry, I can't stop by to see you this time. You, Louise, and the kids take care now, Frankie. Love you.* She remembered the boy who had once hung his arm around Clem's neck in her favorite photograph, who had been buoyed to sleep in the womb of their same mother.

And you too, Eliza, Frank said, his voice gone softer.

The stories we tell ourselves, Clem would have laughed. He had never said a bad word about Frank.

At the Lake Allatoona campsite, Z waved at the small boy, huddled with his knees jutting like heron wings, the thatch of dark hair spiky above his clear forehead. The boy's sideways smile reminded her of so many of the kids she'd taught in schools across the country. Quiet and just looking for some way to express themselves. No matter how much she wanted to save them from adulthood, she couldn't. It would arrive and change them.

Gene, his mother shouted. *Get over here. Now.*

Maybe stranger danger was even more contagious now during COVID-19 times. For all Gene's mother knew, Z could be as violent as Holiday. After all, she was a gray-haired woman wearing all black, even her swimsuit. She was silent, sometimes meditating near the lake's shore on a paddleboard with her eyes closed. An alien thing.

But a sober alien. She remembered her last encounter with Yellow near the lake with Justine and Aakash. She wanted clarity to rid herself of Holiday. Would she ever find Yellow again? Could she ever be Yellow again?

Z watched as Gene sidled up to his brother. They both reached into the same chip bag and didn't look at each other, but they inclined their bodies as if touching. For the first time, she thought of what it might feel like for Yellow to advance across her body: meditative at first, and then a meditation that would push her straight to the edges of herself. And then what would happen?

oOo

Z drove up Highway 75 to Ohio—letting go of her thoughts about Jennifer, snowy owl or great blue heron—a wise bird regardless—toward the site of Holiday's first murder victim: a girl with the name of a bird. Robin, age thirteen. In her school picture in the articles Z looked up online, Robin wore a puka shell necklace and gold granny glasses, popular then. But really, Z thought, passing from Kentucky onto the snarled bridge into Cincinnati, wasn't she going toward the scenes of murder rather than the people themselves?

The word profane kept coming to mind. She was going toward something profane and trying to make it sacred.

At gas station stops, Clem and Holiday kept appearing—but now only in flashes and at a distance, as if receding from direct encounter. Clem's rangy walk. Holiday's face blank behind sunglasses in the car next to her. The sacred and the profane. Clem, beautiful Clem, who had held everything sacred and walked into a hurricane looking for jaguars. And Holiday—throat-crushing Holiday—a mistake of a man.

False binaries, Aakash would say. Aakash, who suddenly felt as lost to her as Clem.

Where are you? she said aloud. He'd asked if she wanted to go with him to India the summer before. Yet, a few weeks before he bought his ticket, he said it was something he wanted to do alone.

Of course, she'd said, her head tilting in the way he tilted his head, but her heart sinking. *Still looking for Anjali?* she wondered.

Art first, she remembered Maude's heavy pronouncement. She laughed now, stalled in Cincinnati's rush hour traffic. Freedom was more like it: something you want for anyone you love. What Maude had called Z's lovecraft had finally been fine-tuned by life, and yet now, the entire world was in lockdown, a total lack of freedom. And she and Aakash on either side of the world.

When she'd stayed at a KOA campground the night before, she'd read in her tent before sleep, taking out the dog-eared Upanishads that Aakash had left on the nightstand. She looked for what he had underlined: *The Self is the ear of the ear, mind of the mind, speech of the speech. He is also breath of the breath, and eye of the eye. Having given up the false identification of the Self with the senses and the mind, and knowing the Self to be Brahman, the wise, on departing this life, become immortal.*

The dream that came to her that night was of Clem walking into the hurricane, hands raised. He'd come to her time and time again, brilliant and as eternal as Yellow. Wintering in black dust, then replenishing, then coming back as thought . . . thought . . . thought.

oOo

Robin Turner had been murdered in 1970, just before the park service took the old amusement park down. Built on the shore in the early 1900s, The Buckeye Lake Amusement Park had a storied past.

The local museum displayed everything with the same fervor, even its hosting of the Ku Klux Klan.

In sepia photographs beneath plastic panels, she saw Ohio's wonders: a crystal ballroom, the Wild Mouse ride, and The Whip. The roller coaster, called the Dips, was the rackety kind and had been abandoned after an accident. According to a wall placard, nobody had been killed on the roller coaster. Next to it, a small newspaper clipping detailed Robin Turner's death.

Robin had run away. Or so her family told *The Columbus Dispatch*. Not one of the good girls Holiday had eventually smothered or drowned. Her nails were full of his flesh; she had hickeys on her neck. Not, the reporter was sure to mention, from the killer.

Z noticed that even during a pandemic, the lake was populated in late June; families packed onto the *Queen of the Lake III*.

Holiday's first kill is how *Unsolved Mysteries* labeled Robin. Her murder made her seem like a deer. A deer caught and slaughtered.

Or shot like the bird of her name. Did she ride the Wild Mouse first at least? Her laugh caught in motion.

Robin was a runaway and, thus, easily overlooked. Dispensable even.

She knew what Clem would say, and Yellow: *It couldn't have been otherwise.*

Z's molestation, Robin's death.

Z kept looking for a reason to stop her heart from its fury, its torment. But the blind allegiance to dull facts at the Greater Buckeye Lake Historical Society Museum and the slut-shaming of Robin Turner made her stomach turn.

She left Buckeye Lake after one night. Robin's face had become a smear of cruel interpretations, of all the ways the victim was not quite who she should have been. Like the unrecovered in New Orleans—the poor and the homeless. Forgotten. Made somehow responsible for their own poverty.

One side loves the other, Yellow had said. But in Earth time, there were the murderers like Holiday. And there were the murderers of the spirit: corrupt institutions, the brunt of a false history.

She'd recovered from Holiday, but she couldn't recover from what he'd done to others. And what others had done to his victims. She couldn't love Holiday.

Perhaps, she worried, couldn't really love.

oOo

Looking back on her car journey, would Z remember where she was when she remembered? When she remembered the mutable woman, the one frozen in ice? Had she usually been tucked under an awning among the bumper cars and the Spider at the state fair? Or was her appearance a one-off, just something outside the Kmart under a haphazard tent where a ticket taker carny-pimp directed you to all the secrets you didn't want to see?

Memory was thick, a trick, she knew, as her car wound its way into the Smokies. Memory came laden with the scent of her mother—now she would call it anise, then licorice, amid the smell of new asphalt, new tar, the blacktop freshly flattened. Her memory was also paved over as she drove into the peel-away real of what appeared to be her present. She remembered the hot sticky summer going into that tented secret—SEE THE WOMAN FROZEN IN ICE! How could it have been just Z and her mother—absent the twins and her sisters with their chlorine-green hair—had she and her mother gone to Kmart alone?

Could a drone see her now as she traveled in Aakash's Karmann Ghia away from Buckeye Lake, away from the sites of death, away from the murders? Away from the figments of Holiday and Clem?

From Z's height as a girl, she couldn't look down on the woman in her black maillot; she had to raise herself on tiptoe to see over the rim of the steely tub, so like a coffin, where the woman lay flat, her arms locked to her sides, her eyes closed. Or were they open? She was fathoms deep in ice: a detail Z can't fathom now.

SEE, the carny said, IT'S NOT A TRICK, MELINDA IS VERY MUCH ALIVE. Did Z make up the name *Melinda*? Her black hair did not snake from her head like a mermaid's in a tub. She was a young woman, not beautiful, just plain; she wore a one-piece, coal black, her lips a slight blue. For years, had Melinda risen from some deep well of Z's mind as she slept? COME SEE THE WOMAN FROZEN IN ICE?

Her mother's presence, her scent, was part of the real, but the carny's liquid form, his surly dirty secret—a woman alive, yet frozen in ice. Years later, before her mother died, Z had phoned to ask her if she'd dreamed it—*Was it true? Did we go together?* Silence as the line clicked with small noises as lines used to do. *Yes*, her mother said. *I remember it too.*

Z asked, *How did she breathe?*

But her mother, she remembered, as she watched the yellow line disappear under her car, was vague, unclear. Neither of them could remember the secret of the trick—how a woman could be alive but frozen, divested of breath, locked deep.

How did she do it? Z asked again.

As the line clicked and popped, Z took another turn on the road, remembering that her mother said, *Easy. It's easy.*

Another turn. Now that she's driving, as usual, into the backcountry of the real, the cell tower drops her connection. Alone again. It's easy. Until it's not.

oOo

Heading up into the Smoky Mountains, taking the back roads, Z only wanted to retreat from the human. On the dashboard's console, in a black divot, one of Aakash's bracelets shook and bounced like one of the old rosaries that she'd been gifted for Mass. A Buddha's head instead of a cross. She never remembered Aakash wearing it, yet it had always been here: the eyes of the Buddha closed in prayer. *The Self is the ear of the ear, mind of the mind, speech of the speech. He is also breath of the breath, and eye of the eye.* The phrases, as if traveling from Aakash's head into hers, tapped themselves out on the console.

The roads began to seem illusory, unreal, the thread of the center line as if pulling her into the mountains, pulling her towards something she always knew was there. She didn't want to see the faces anymore: Jennifer's, Robin's, Holiday's. She would forgo her last two destinations: Mary Grace and Donna who were murdered in Kentucky lakes.

She did not want to startle again at Clem's vagrant face.

She did not want to see her own. She would set up camp as deep in the woods as she could find. Maybe there she could become less real to herself or more real. She wasn't sure which. She headed toward Gatlinburg where she got a backcountry permit, cool prickles of fear replaced by something steely: her resolve. She stopped at an REI afterwards. The young woman helping her made sure Z's pack was light but filled with everything she would need.

I don't want to hike too far, Z heard herself say, *just, you know, to be alone, to immerse myself in the woods, see how long I can be there. Amid,* she raised her hands, as if letting out sparks, *it all.*

The young woman's long face and dark eyes, like a whippet, nodded, then she smiled. Or at least Z thought she smiled behind her mask. A zebra pattern obscured her nose and mouth—black and white stripes.

You're a Panpsychic, right?

A what?

Oh, you know, kinda a seeker? Looking for pan—all of it—and psyche or mind, spirit—in everything? I'm doing that myself this summer. The girl turned from her to hunt down the next item Z would need.

In the parked car, newly loaded with her supplies, she looked up *Panpsychism* on her phone and saw an article published just last January, before the pandemic had shut down the world. Two *pans*—two kinds of alls, she thought.

Does Consciousness Pervade the Universe? the author asked. *Why, yes*, Z said aloud, looking blankly past her steering wheel and into the mountains on the horizon where she was headed. Instead, the feeling of wonder she'd had the summer she was twelve rippled through her chest like the pseudopods of Yellow's advancing tendrils.

The salesgirl who had helped her was another of the young people, like Justine, that Z felt were way ahead of her generation. Another new young one ready to take on something bigger than the material world. Her name was Callie, light on her feet and balancing on one leg as she bagged Z's purchases. She had appeared like a wood sprite. Arriving in Z's life, as all things and all people had, just when she was ready for them.

Of course, it had been easy, on mushrooms, to tap back into Yellow's consciousness. To find that cyclical and beautiful thought that had come in the form of the voice and appearance of Clem. The words she had somewhat forgotten now—but the knowledge of the inner space and the outer space—Clem and Pete, metaphors for pure thought—had stayed with her.

But often, they were just that—metaphors—not something she lived. Everyday life in lockdown, especially everyday life without Aakash, had worn at her. She set up camp in a hollow Callie had circled on the map. Less than half a mile away, she'd told Z, was an overlook where the mountains spread out below. She was right. Z walked to the outcropping where she looked at the mountains veined with sand-colored earth and furred by the breathing animate trees like an immense body lushly rippling and waiting for something to happen.

oOo

When just the last of the apricot sun lingered over the rolling mountains on the horizon, Z walked back to her campsite in the hollow. She had built the fire after setting up her tent and would light it when she returned. At the store, she'd bought the packets called Mystical Fire that the wood sprite had pointed out to her.

These will make your campfire psychedelic, Callie said, her eyes widening over her zebra mask. Even with her flashlight, Z's way back in the dark took on the accretion of the real again. Had she ever been in the dark woods by herself like this? Yes, that time at the residency when she'd been with Yellow. But it had been a short walk to her cabin, and Aakash and Justine had known where she was all along. Now, the songbirds that filled the woods at dusk had quieted. Other, more mysterious, sounds erected their little structures.

Once lit, the colorful fire did invite her in—a preamble for the mystical for sure. Z held up her metal cup with its weak herbal tea to toast Callie. There was no pattern to the dance—sometimes orange, sometimes red, numerous shades of blue and purple were there, a lick of green. The dance, she thought, was endless, ongoing, and risky at every turn.

She wished Aakash was with her, and Z let her mind float over the ocean to where he may be, but it was too far and their connection too thin now for her to feel him. She'd put herself apart from everything here. Maybe it was easy—far from civilization—to forget the murderers of the innocents, to forget about the sacred and the profane. Maybe it was easy to think it all sacred. Maybe to think, she resigned herself, was the problem.

Was she safe? She wasn't sure. Her resolve floundered amid the unknown noises around her. Leaves rustled in the trees across from her. Branches popped. A slight scraping noise. She let her mind go blank into the moment—closing her eyes so that her Smoky Mountain campsite, attended by the smell of burning wood, became her habitation.

Safe, I'm safe, she whispered, trying to will her body to calmness.

When she opened her eyes again, she saw the source of the noises opposite her. A dark form was slowly descending the oak tree on the other side of the fire. A bear. A black bear.

She remembered what they'd told her at the visitor's center: *Don't approach a bear. If a bear approaches you, make yourself big. Don't play dead.*

But the bear didn't seem to notice her at all. It appeared to be heading toward the small portable cooler she'd left on the ground, that she hadn't yet hung from the tree like she was supposed to.

Damn, too short to hang my shit! And not big enough to make myself bigger. Her bear spray was in the pack, and her pack was in the tent. She sat paralyzed, making excuses to only herself. Had she breathed yet?

The bear easily turned over the cooler and a cylinder of cookies rolled out. The bear's rounded form wasn't too large, maybe 170 pounds. A female, then. And it was mating season, of course. But the bear was occupied with trying to get the packet opened. Z almost wanted to help her, until the bear looked a little sideways.

She had known Z was there watching all along. The firelight caught the bear's eye, turning it into cod liver oil. Wasn't the oily light reflected in Holiday's aviator frames the same? The same vitreous shield: no way in.

The profane. To be profaned. To profane. How awful to have to hide from yourself all the time. That's what Holiday had done, was probably doing right now. To make himself bigger, to protect himself from the truth of his own existence. To hurt and suffocate girls was to hurt and to try to suffocate himself. Because his ego was so easily wounded and to kill was to make the self substantial to himself? Yes, to make himself more real, instead of a thing in a world without substance.

The compassion she had for Holiday crystallized, just as Jennifer's face had crystallized. The bear swatted at the packet and ripped it open with her mouth. The appearance of the bear was like the night: furred and interior. The smell of the bear was like the wood smoke, was like a wildness that flared up inside her. She was the bear, now crunching, now licking at the fallen crumbs.

Z gritted her teeth, trying to impede the next thought: if she was the bear, then she was Holiday too.

She took a breath, finally, and her lungs opened like wings in the even dark as she sighed deeply. The bear knew she sat on the other side of night's circle, heard her sigh, but didn't appear to mind. Without fuel, the fire was dying down, and the bear swatted at the cooler again, but it was empty. Everything else was on her side of the fire, and Z realized they had an understanding between them. Their shadows, here, may overlap, but they could still be distinct.

The embers glowed an orange, a yellow, an orange, a yellow—the colors stripped away to the essential. The bear lumbered away from the circle and into the woods without looking back, so Z did not see the wavering cod liver eyes again. The bear's rolling hide in the darkness nothing but the fear of the other. Or the other as the self.

She looked up at the sheer wonder of the stars. There were so many, and they punctured and enflamed all her wishes. Profane and sacred collapsed in the brittle movie of her life and she was thankful.

One side loves the other as the other. Maybe that was the rest that Yellow had been trying to tell her all along.

oOo

She didn't let the bear scare her away. Why would she leave now? They had come to the edges of each other. She stayed four more days until her food ran out, using the compact hatchet Callie put on her list to chop wood. She hiked the trails that appeared like spokes from her campsite and walked to the creek bed one evening as the sun set.

Across from her on the other bank, a large oak tree had wound its exposed roots as if sitting lotus-style, and she sat marveling at its poised beauty.

Dusk deepened around the tree, and at first just a whisper of fireflies began, an even bleating in the just-darkness. But they gathered, thickened, and their yellow throbs had a beat, a meter. Their show was luminous, *cinematic*, as Pete might say—a flutter of sparks, followed by an even lighting for ten to fifteen seconds, then they would cease. To a slow count of four to five seconds: the silence, the rest, the void, then once more erratic sparks like murmurs starting, until the fireflies lit all at once, the space around her brilliant with dense stars. Was this what Pete felt—rolling out to the ends of his tether and into space?

Like poetry, yet more than poetry. Across the banks, their show was a conscious synchronous illumination as thousands of fireflies lit. She turned and saw that they were everywhere, all around her. She held her breath when they fired all together, as if awakened into a multi-dimensional universe, then breathed out when they extinguished themselves.

The fireflies reminded her of the faeries that had flown at her face that distant summer. Could they have been fireflies? Now she knew that *Panpsychic* means everything is conscious—just as Yellow is. But then, could it also be an illusion? No, and yes.

She remembered the faeries had carried the freight of war at first. As if they'd become those stilled army figures that the twins had left in the rain. Only after they had fired their weapons, releasing everything that was ugly, had they carried a harvest of peace, beauty, and tactile sensation. The eternal cycle of opposites: evil and good, life and death, a me and a you. How would we know one without the other?

Now—aging and earthbound—she was almost the same self she had been at twelve, standing in a boundless field of light, a figment among dramatic figments: yellow, yellow, yellow—showing themselves in an endless stream of what she knew as infinite love. And she was them, and she was that.

oOo

The next day, as Z wound her way down the mountainside, her screen lit up with a text from Aakash on WhatsApp. He'd written it two days ago.

Been in hospital. Here in Rajasthan. Don't want you to worry. Just a flirtation with the virus, I think. LOL.

He actually wrote *LOL*. He never wrote *LOL*. And what the hell did *flirtation* mean?

Z pulled up at a rest stop.

LOL? She wrote. *I've been out of range. I'm sorry. Please call.*

No need to worry. I'm pulling through. Too tired to talk. The sobs broke over her like a storm she'd been waiting for. Maybe she'd known it all along, had been driving not just to make peace with Holiday, but to escape from the inevitable. She drove without resting all the way back to the REI parking lot in Gatlinburg. She locked the car doors and tried to sleep in the backseat but kept opening the Upanishads, looking for the lines Aakash had underlined.

He who realizes the existence of Brahman behind every activity of his being—whether sensing, perceiving, or thinking—he alone gains immortality. Through knowledge of Brahman comes power. Through knowledge of Brahman comes victory over death.

oOo

Pandemic Timeline

January 2020: Scientist in China confirms a mysterious new pneumonia-like illness identified in Wuhan in December 2019 can be transmitted from human to human

Researchers later determine first appearance of SARS-CoV-2 in Hubei, China, that had probably already spread globally by January

China's first official COVID-19 case located and linked to Wuhan's Huanan seafood market; However, early cases had no known connection with Huanan, indicating SARS-CoV-2 already circulated before it reached the market

China puts Wuhan under strict lockdown

On the other side of the globe, the US sees its first official case of the disease, later named COVID-19; Patient is a Washington state resident and traveled to Wuhan

February 2020: Cases of COVID-19 begin to multiply around the world; Countries restrict travel to contain the virus

March 2020: World Health Organization (WHO) characterizes COVID-19 as a pandemic

In the United States, the Grand Princess cruise ship is held at sea off the coast

of California after twenty-one of 3,500 people aboard test positive for the virus; California also becomes the first state to order all residents to stay

home with the exception of going to an

essential job or shopping for essential needs

Hospitals become overwhelmed at the rise in cases; nationwide shortage of personal protective equipment (PPE)

Trump Administration declares public health emergency
Businesses shut down, leading to massive job losses, schools close for online instruction, sporting events canceled, and college students go home

April 2020: Cases continue to surge; countries keep borders sealed
People start wearing masks and practicing "social distancing"

May 2020: Experts focus on "flattening the curve." After months in lockdown, due to economic concerns, states slowly begin phased reopening based on criteria outlined by Trump Administration, in coordination with state, county, and local officials; Meanwhile, scientists across the globe race to understand the disease, to find treatments and solutions, and to develop vaccines

May 28—US COVID-19 deaths pass the 100,000 mark

June 2020: Efforts to reopen the economy lead to new cases; curve is not flattening; Experts point to dangers of large gatherings and use terms like "clusters" and "super-spreader" events

Worldwide: 503,862 deaths

oOo

The contagion had escaped his notice, had become merely a minor inconvenience. By the time Aakash was in Rajasthan, India—waiting for the van to take him to the bottom of the Ramgarh Crater—he barely thought of it. Since he'd come to India, he'd tried to stay absorbed in each moment. He looked for the images that appeared lit from within.

And from nothing, they appeared. As now, in front of him, the fruit sellers in their roadside stall. Occasionally, a swath of multicolored fabric caught the wind, and he saw the sinewy figures of the grandparents, twisted together on mats to the rear of the stall, occasionally coughing.

He took a bite of the mango he'd bought from the wrinkled woman, perhaps their daughter. She had aged before her time. He'd pared the skin with a knife, its deep orange flesh sweet and soothing in his mouth. Mango smelling of mango, tasting of mango.

The sheet they had on the makeshift hovel fell back again. The veiled.

The further into the country he ventured, the more his project had morphed into something else altogether. His project was no longer about Indian women. It wasn't about what they did and did not disclose behind their veils. Instead, he'd begun to think his photographs were about the mysteries that we hide from in everyday life. The photos he captured tended toward the fragmentary, the overlooked. Amid the riot of honking horns and blurred lights, he had captured the lone cow standing unperturbed, its near luminescent hide swirled like a dervish of understanding.

He wanted to tell Z about how his project had changed, wished, often, that she'd come with him. Now and again, he had thought of sending her a ticket, but something deeper put a hand to his hand. The gesture that said, *Wait, just wait.* She'd been fine with his decision to go alone; he'd worked out that, of course, she had her own projects—what interest did she have in India? When he finally booked his ticket, he sensed that his adventure had something conclusive in it, and once he arrived in late March, the news was that the contagion, COVID-19, had hit worldwide. Maybe that was it? Maybe they both knew it wasn't her time to leave home.

At the insistence of his parents, he initially stayed with friends of theirs in Mumbai, but after a week, Aakash decided to travel anyway. Their comfortable lifestyle could be seductive; he was long past the pull of seduction and a contagion wouldn't interfere with his seeking. Now it was just a part of what he sought. In the countryside, few wore masks and most didn't. Everyone, in the beginning anyway, before the police ordered them home, still packed the local markets and the trains.

He'd come to the crater with purpose, once he'd heard of it. As often happened in India, you talked to the strangers with the light-filled eyes on the packed buses where people swayed together or in a market stall once you told them why you were traveling. He often let native Indians such as Pramod, whom he had met on a bus in Mumbai, wearing an ebullient smile, guide his next step.

You must see the crater at Rajasthan, my hometown, Pramod had pronounced. *It is four kilometers across. A wonder you should not miss.*

Now, sitting behind the driver on the rutted road, Aakash checked the digital image on his camera's screen. His photograph had caught the fabric's rosy blur like an eyelid opening to reveal the aged couple on the mats, clinging to each other. Were their eyes beholding the other? They were part of each other, Aakash already knew.

The van departed with the churning of sand and stones, and once they traveled down and disembarked, he walked to the Bhand Deva temple, made entirely of sandstone and layered with carvings—most of amorous couples, typical of Khajuraho architecture. A fine green film of moss shadowed the sculptures, and vines hung from the joists in the ceiling. The eroding copulating couples carved into the walls and in the pillars elicited giggles from two small girls who hurried in and out, playing hide and seek.

Aakash smiled and sat down on his backpack, looking up into the sandstone ceiling: such a play of geometrics. Circles within a hexagon within a square. Birds flew in and out of the structure, their sounds echoing. The oculus, that compelling opening at the center of the ceiling, was the navel of the universe. What Pramod had said: a navel at the center of a crater that had been created by an asteroid hurtling through space over one thousand million years ago.

Pramod told him that new theories said that life had been distributed throughout space all along and that the meteorite that struck the Earth to create the crater carried interstellar grains that could even have initiated life on our planet.

They ate together a few days ago, before they parted, and as usual, Aakash thought that meeting Pramod felt like a fascinating trail that he had no choice but to follow. It wasn't luck; it was about listening to and following the signs.

Panspermia, Pramod had said, tearing the naan and dipping it into the small dish of *daal* served near his own.

What is that? Aakash asked.

Greek, Pramod said, nodding. *Pan is all, as you know. And sperma or seed. Life*, he held out a finger like a candle, *exists throughout the universe and disperses everywhere. Who knows what microorganisms could even have come to Earth on a spacecraft, and who knows what will become of them?*

Yellow, Aakash thought. He would text Z and tell her about Pramod and panspermia.

But he'd forgotten to text before he lost cell service, and later, it didn't seem necessary.

He took photographs: one he liked especially was a long exposure of the girls going around a pillar. Their hide and seek game stretched into a band of color hovering in space—just what this whole dream was about. He felt the warmth of that scene, felt its poignancy, as illusory as his own eyes, watching them. As illusory as the camera that captured their flight.

After the few other tourists who had taken the van down with him to the site left, he built a small fire within the circle of stones where others before him had warmed up their Indian lunches.

After he ate, he walked back to the tantric temple to Shiva, vowing to take it in—beautiful and ruined, like a breathing thing. A small pond at the temple's base reflected the pillars with their thick vines speckled with light.

He looked at the now-rosy scar on his inner arm rarely, but when he did, he remembered the inside of death. Remembered it held no fear for him. He'd gone into death's crater, and he remembered the wonder, the just-gasp of a great beauty before the EMTs had pulled him out of the bathtub.

When he'd told Z about his near-death experience, she asked, *But does it stop there? Is that when you came to what you know now?*

No, he told her. *It was just the turning point. That's when I had to dig in and question everything. What's real and what's not?*

Turning his forearm to the sun, sitting near the pond, a great calm rippled through him. A calm he could enter when he closed his eyes and went to the stillness. He'd hurt Anjali; that was his only regret.

He decided he could ascend to the smaller temples in the morning. He could walk the 750 steps, the harried van driver had said, to the two smaller temples dedicated to two goddesses. Something unveiled. He hadn't brought anything for breakfast, but he was barely hungry anymore.

That evening, he meditated until he lost track of time at the bottom of a crater under the navel, amid deities dancing, amid humans dancing. In a temple to Shiva—Auspicious One, Destroyer.

Aakash never liked to make one moment better than another. But this one, how could it not be a pinnacle? Under the geometric roof, at first his breathing became more than his own until his spine gently pulsed, then vibrated, rippling from the bottom of the crater up into his *muladhara*. The breathing was the light that traveled up through his head, and he was filled with the throb that shot out and up through the round circle—like a keyhole—into something everyone would call space but that Aakash felt was eternity. Gradually he came back to the night sounds around him. He did not know that he had been crying with an unnamed joy.

He moved back near the fire to sleep amid the scrub trees and the pond lapping in the small pool. That night at the center of the crater, the erotic couples inhabited his dreams, an entire orgy—the play of their bodies arousing his body to the figments of Anjali and Z, and then the slow and beautiful melding of all their bodies. He woke sometime in the night and laughed aloud into the spiraling stars overhead.

oOo

He waited at the place where the van had dropped him off the previous morning, meditating in the milky light. His stomach growled, but he felt the utter calm of his evening at Bhand Deva.

The driver stopped to pick up a family at the side of the road on their way back to Rajasthan. Aakash was just getting service again, so he looked up on his phone the meaning of the symbolism of all those copulating humans in Khajuraho temples.

Moksha, he read, *the state which is like a man and woman in close embrace—it means the final release or reunion between two principles—the essence—Purusha—and nature—Prakriti.*

The family around him laughed together; the father balanced a small boy on his knee, who leaned over him to look out the window. There, he saw a trail of goats keeping pace with the van. The man leaned heavily against him, chattering to his family, all of them grinning.

Something felt slightly off, and Aakash realized that he was sweating, and everyone else was too, and yet he couldn't smell a thing.

He smiled at the family and at the goats running alongside, kicking up clouds of dust. He remembered a question from the Upanishads that was not a question: *For him who sees everywhere oneness, how can there be delusion or grief.*

oOo

We protect ourselves from the truth all the time. Sometimes through simple erasure. Like Nixon's tapes. Like Haig, Nixon's chief of staff, whose bigger lie about the erasure was more truthful than even he could understand. Eighteen plus minutes of silence: the power of attachments and our futile will to erase that truth.

We protect ourselves from truth all the time. Sometimes through simple pleasures.

Did the *sinister force* emanate from him or from All? Is the story bound to happen anyway, despite what we obscure or omit? What truths do we run from?

Yellow didn't escape, though that's what Z had told herself for a long time. It was only now that she fully realized what her mother had done. And why she'd tried to forget.

PART III

oooоOoooo

Summer's traceries would never be lived again, or so I thought. My body gave in to womanhood. By late July, I'd gotten my period. The hard knots under my breasts that had been my armor unwound. My breasts puckered out, blooming like small dark roses. Cheryl and Janice shot their old bras like slingshots at me before bedtime. They tucked tampon cylinders under my pillow with notes: *Get used to me for the rest of your life*, one said, and, *I will live in your vagina, and you will hate me.*

But I thought myself different; maybe I had no reason to, but I did.

The faeries had appeared to me. I'd felt myself floating amid goddesses in The House of Voodoo. Yellow and Clem had been my constant companions. We looked up into the heavens, and Clem told me about Skylab. We knew possibility and entryways. I didn't want womanhood, didn't want what the man at the lake had tried to make of me. Couldn't I still be a girl, or even a girl-boy, if I wanted?

But I couldn't erase how everything changed and by a subterfuge.

My mother had gotten all three of us excited for it—the art class at the library. *Ages eight to twelve*, she'd said. *Exactly your ages. You'll have the best time.*

My mother was distracted when we got ready. I'd overheard the news blaring from the television earlier in the morning after my father had turned up the dial. *Top Story Today*, an announcer said. *Judge Sirica orders President Nixon to hand over nine tapes recorded on the private White House taping system.*

My father muttered, *Jesus H. Christ. They've been asking him to turn them over for a damn month!*

Burt, my mother said to him. *Do not take the Lord's name in vain!*

The president had recorded something that he didn't want anyone else to hear. He had secrets, as I did. As, I was soon to learn, my mother did too.

At the art class, the teacher wanted us to use any of the materials from what she called her magic box to reimagine our summer. Esther was the art teacher's name. A herd of sweaty kids huddled together on the floor and only two others my age sat at a round table. One was a bespectacled boy, the other a girl in a wheelchair with a lopsided grin. The three of us waited while the kids went nuts over Esther's magic box, leaving a trail of sequins, torn strips from wallpaper books, feathers, and raffia. I watched Frank grab coils of string—black and bright yellow—and I knew that even though the Saints didn't play in the summer, he was going to somehow demonstrate his year-round fandom. Clem got lost in the shuffle, and I didn't see what he'd found. When our turn came, the girl in the wheelchair asked me to choose anything for her since she couldn't reach it.

Oh, let's take our time; let me help you, Esther said to her—patting me on the shoulder. As I scavenged for anything yellow—ripped lace, small seed-sized bugle beads, a spray of tulle—I overheard Esther's calm voice and peered at her waft of straight dark hair and the eagerness of her hands as she bent to help the girl make something.

To make something, that's what I wanted. Like Esther did. Esther was who I could be— the thought almost passed through me and out again. A passing thought. But a blush of heat rose up through my body, riveting up and out of my head, as if a signal from Yellow for me to listen.

Oh, I smiled. I wanted to tell my mother who had asked me at Café du Monde over a month ago what I wanted to be when I grew up. The thin art teacher with the patient voice, the lines around her eyes just showing. That's me.

I stitched the yellow tulle with a needle and thread while everyone else used too much glue; one girl started licking the paste, and Esther had a librarian call her mother. When it was my turn to show what I'd made, Esther rested her warm hand on the nape of my neck as she'd done with everyone else. Across the circle, I saw Clem beaming at me. I had no idea how he'd found the accordion plastic tubing that he'd connected from a paper airplane to a little figure he'd made out of a white sock, but I knew he'd be telling everyone about Skylab.

It was my turn now. I wasn't sure there was a thing I could tell them. Because I had no language for it. The children's eyes burned into my lowered head.

I've never seen something so fantastical, Esther said. *How incredible. Eliza, what does this tell us about your summer?*

I looked up at her. *It looks like it doesn't exist,* I said, *but I found something just like it in my backyard.*

Is it a flower? Esther asked. *A mushroom?*

Something like that, I said. *But . . . it's kinda like everything too.* I heard a boy snicker from a place I couldn't see, but the teacher's gentle hand went soft at my neck as if reassuring me.

That's an experience I hope everyone has one day, Esther said.

oooo〇oooo

Yellow couldn't have escaped. Yellow didn't escape.

After the art class, my mother looked angry. She motioned us to hurry into the station wagon with her cigarette wagging.

How'd it go? she asked, shifting the car into reverse.

Mama, Clem scooted up from the backseat, his mouth almost in my mother's ear. *The art teacher liked Eliza's the best!*

I thought, *She did?*

Good grief, Clem—why are you yelling in my ear? Sit down and fasten your seat belt, Mama said. Frank farted.

Haha, he laughed. *Eliza was teacher's pet.*

I looked down: on my lap sprawled the even spread of my version of Yellow. The bugle beads glinted, and my mother frowned at it.

Look at that, she said. *What do you know.*

Mama, I began, because I wanted to tell her that now I knew the answer to her question. I would be an artist and a teacher. She'd asked me, and I knew it now.

Listen, she interrupted, staring at the road ahead. *I don't want you to be surprised. Clem told me about that mess of crap out on the log, and I didn't tell your dad about it, so you can thank me for that. But it looked dangerous. Toxic! That's what I told the people at the lab.*

My mouth slackened, filling with saliva.

What do you mean the lab? I said.

I called the university. Biology Department. I could have called the parish waste disposal, but I thought maybe someone has a use for it. Who knew they'd pay me for it? She tapped her cigarette ash out the open window.

My whole chest felt frozen, and I wanted to turn around and swat Clem's legs, but even from where I sat, I felt Clem sinking low in the backseat.

Mama, what did you do? I suddenly wailed. She smacked my legs hard.

Do not start, Eliza.

I'd never once started anything, I thought, gulping. Ever. The fake Yellow on my lap suddenly looked like that. Fake. I wadded it up between my hands, smelling the stink of my mother's cigarette hanging in the car, the stink of her mouth. She sold Yellow.

The money will help with your school uniforms, she said. *That man said he'd never really seen anything like it. I guess they'll do tests on it. That mister acted like it was the best thing since sliced bread.*

It is, I muttered.

What did you say, young lady?

I said that it is. They are! But it wasn't yours to take, Mama.

Do you own this house? she said, jabbing her finger when we pulled up in the driveway. *Eliza?* But I'd already slammed the car door, throwing down the stupid art project and letting it trail behind me on the driveway.

When I ran to the backyard, there was nothing. Not a shred of Yellow who had grown so big that they had overtaken the log. I banged my arms along the dead torso of the tree screaming and screaming. I had never screamed so loud. When Clem came too close to me, I yelled at him as my mother had yelled at me.

I told you not to Clem. I told you not to—remember what I said?

His head could not have hung lower. He mumbled something over and over.

What are you saying? What are you saying? I shook his little frame by the shoulders until his teeth clacked together. Clem had picked my art project from the driveway, and it slid from his hands as I shook him. He was crying too.

I thought she would love Yellow like we do. I thought, I thought, I thought she needed them too, I shouted.

But she didn't need them, did she? She didn't.

My face must have been frightening because his lips trembled as my lips trembled, and I said it so he'd remember.

Remember what I said, Clem? You told her, and now she might die!

oooOoooo

It was simple. Because everything is. When Kerwin and Conrad stood up, when the hinge popped, Kerwin went one way, Conrad the other.

Falling and ascending—Earth's horizon filling mind end to end—seeing the sun's sudden flares for the first time, twisting 25,000 miles wide.

Ascending and falling into no mind. Everything that tethers is nothing, no thing.

At the end of the umbilical, Conrad's eyes filled with one unquenchable joy. Until he was not Conrad at all but seeing as we all see Conrad, his unquenchable joy. His story: *If you can't be good, be colorful*, his mother said with her rich laugh.

Falling: his rage when he could not read the words on a page as a kid. Ascending: his mother's warm arms, his son's eyes as he died. Falling now into that space, a space so infinite that he cannot stop laughing. His story. The stories.

Yellow came to be—but where? Among planets, spinning as Conrad did—Newton's first law? Spinning and weightless because gravity is the first illusion.

It was simple: everything is. Yellow, what Conrad witnessed as he fell through the sun.

Yellow takes shape—one single cell, numerous nuclei, 360 possible combinations, their pseudopods stretching and engulfing, Yellow finds their flourishing—a consciousness never embodied, but wholly the body . . .

oooоOoooo

There was always the possibility I might come completely undone. The possibility arrived as an image—a well-used nest when the twigs decompose, when the molted feathers rot, when I would simply return to matter.

Or if I was just energy, as Aakash always said, then all of my filaments, like delicate rainbows, may separate, and I will be glad to be no more.

How unexpected and yet expected, my thoughts spoke as I drove toward Justine's house in Asheville. That he had gotten sick. That he was sick so far away.

I had called Justine the morning after receiving Aakash's text, knowing that, with COVID-19 infections on the rise, what I asked of her would be difficult. Yet, I just couldn't face going home and seeing remnants of Aakash everywhere.

You can stay in our guest house, Justine said, when I told her of Aakash's illness. *You'll need to quarantine first, but our home is your home. I can't imagine the waiting, Z!*

I'd been right those years ago—Justine had found a beloved even more loving than her first husband. Bryson, the high school biology teacher where Justine taught music. Along with her more esoteric tastes, Justine loved R&B, and he loved bluegrass. Aakash and I had danced at their wedding reception in an old barn to a band that played all the music they loved. Now there was Fern, only five months old. Because of Fern's birth, Justine had been spared the spring of Zoom classes, and now they were both on summer break.

What was love? I thought, taking the long way through Tennessee—*but another filament—an invisible energy as breakable as glass.*

Don't go, Aakash, I whispered into the windshield as the Buddha's head throbbed on the dashboard. As previously I'd seen the faces of the dual—Clem and Holiday—the sacred and the profane—now the color yellow began to distill before me in the landscape. A yellow house on the rise of a hill, rolled bundles of new hay spaced apart like monstrous caterpillars.

Love was a glass, a window, a mirror. Love was a multiplicity of forms. Or was it just one giant thing, like Yellow? Love caught in my chest like a pulsing moth—its wings beating against my heart and in my throat, trapped.

Aakash's texts, I knew, were designed to ease my mind, but they were also inconclusive. *Everything will be as it should be, dear one; What wondrous next steps!* and probably the most ominous: *Keep present in the moment . . .*

When I stopped to camp in Hot Springs, North Carolina, I remembered our travel to Santorini many summers ago. How we swam to a flat rock and soaked up the sun, silently. Though we both fell asleep, I was always dimly aware of how his dark limbs tangled with mine. His spicy scent—cloves and cardamom—was sometimes my scent too, and the dark hairs on his chest under my fingers were like the fibers of my being.

Don't go, I chanted as I drove. I remembered the bear's glinting eyes—the invisible boundary between us—and how I had recognized myself in that eye.

Aakash bathed in sunlight.

Aakash sleeping while I walked around the apartment, his eyes dreaming under his closed lids.

Aakash said things no one else did. When Aakash spoke, people drew nearer to him.

Aakash's feline grace that I'd seen from the beginning.

Aakash's stitched-together arm meant he'd been opened wide and thank god, he would never close to life again. Unless he had to.

Yellow daisies filled fields with each turn on a mountain pass.

Sunflowers swayed in a backyard with a rotting jungle gym. And all along, that yellow line under my car propelled me onward and onward.

oooo0oooo

The summer days in Asheville would have seemed idyllic if they weren't about waiting.

During quarantine, Justine and Bryson talked to me through the half-opened glass storm door to the guesthouse and set food in small crocks on a tray. Bryson was the cook in the family, and Justine often brought the tray back and forth for meals. She sat cross-legged on the grass in front of the door, joggling Fern on her knee. The small girl with a moon-sized head of curls would sit placidly until she became aware of the strange specter of my face behind the glass. Slowly, her velvet eyes would widen, her forehead would wrinkle, and she'd begin to cry. I must have appeared to her like a trapped animal. All the resolve from my journey had withered, and I felt exactly like a trapped animal.

Day five of the quarantine when the call came. I bolted awake in the middle of the night to the jangling tone of my iPhone, the volume always on. I dimly realized that it was the next day in the Rajasthan hospital where Aakash had been for two weeks.

The moth in my chest quaked and battered as I sat up in bed, a hand to my throat, and pressed the button to accept the call.

It was a video call: the reception delayed and grainy. Like my dread-laden imaginings, it was everything I didn't want it to be. But it was Aakash.

He was behind one of those horrifying face masks, with a nozzle like an alien. The sound of the ventilator—the machine for the living breath—dominated the call as if everything had been reduced to that mechanical sound. The nurse spoke English carefully, cradling Aakash's sweat-soaked head and holding Aakash's phone so I could see them both. But her words were muffled under a mask and goggles, her hair tucked under a mushroom-shaped hat, her hands gloved.

I was trapped in the vortex of the image, concentrating and yet almost frozen. Later, I felt like it was a dream, but an indelible one I would never forget.

He says he loves you very much, the nurse said, looking at a piece of paper.

He says he is at peace. He wrote here, her head cocked as if not understanding, *know I am in you, as you are part of me.*

He wrote—Aakash's eyes were not blurry, they were widened and bulging under the mask as if he was holding onto my image as I was to his. *To know it*—the nurse looked down at her notes, her wrist shaking—*to know it all—as yellow. Be present with yellow.*

Then he finally blinked. No, he wasn't just blinking, his eyes were glassing over, losing their ability to see; the beautiful mast of his eyes were closing on me, and I heard my own rough intake of breath and my rushing words, as if there were no time left in the world:

I love you, Aakash; I want to be there, to hold you. And I . . . I hear what you're saying . . . I know what you mean, I know . . . I trailed off as the wet strafed my face. He struggled once more to open his eyes.

It wasn't right. What I said to him. It wasn't enough. I was tangled in the sheets, sweat poured from my body, and as he leaned his head back, I watched his Adam's apple go up and down, and then wobble, and his head nodded *yes.*

Then his eyes, half-mast, looked up at something beyond my image on the phone's screen. The machine's sound had taken over, taken over everything, was the only thing clicking and exhaling, exhaling, exhaling.

Elongated minutes watching his eyes lose Aakash, long enormous minutes when I touched the small screen as if willing my fingers to go through to the self, leaving the self.

All that was left was to look again at the nurse's face.

I am sorry, she said. *He was an exceptionally fine man. Everyone has grown to care for him very much here.* Her head dropped into her hand.

He *was.*

I don't remember saying goodbye. The screen that had contained the form of Aakash went dark.

My face was pressed to the mattress. I had to remember, had to remember the Aakash that did not fear death. I beat a powerless fist on the mattress. Like Clem, Aakash knew himself in everything.

Against my closed lids, I saw the flash of Manet's *Dead Christ,* the painting I had visited so often at the Met as a young woman. There was the angel with my face wearing the saffron-colored robe. I remembered the other angel too, with her head in her hands, like Aakash's nurse.

When barely twenty, I had recognized Aakash's face. The eyes holding nothing, his palms upright.

oooo0oooo

Pandemic Timeline

July 2020: Pandemic causes uptick in mental health issues as job losses continue to soar, parents juggle working at home with caring for or homeschooling children, and young adults grow frustrated by isolation from friends and limited job prospects; Officials debate best scenarios for allowing children to safely return to school in the fall

August 2020: First documented case of reinfection reported in Hong Kong; COVID-19 now third leading cause of death in the US

September 2020: School year opens with a mix of plans to keep children and teachers safe, from in-person classes to remote schooling to hybrid models
Centers for Disease Control and Prevention (CDC) reports that people recently positive were about twice as likely to report dining at a restaurant than those with negative test results

September 28: In ten months, death toll from COVID-19 is more than one million worldwide

October 2020: President Trump tests positive for COVID-19 after White House Rose Garden gathering—multiple people also infected; Food and Drug Administration (FDA) grants full approval to a drug called remdesivir for treatment of COVID-19

October 6: US food insecurity rises to fifty-two million people as a result of the COVID-19 pandemic—seventeen million more people than pre-pandemic numbers.

November 2020: Cases surge due to cold weather; the US begins to break records for daily cases/deaths; Many officials around the country bring plans for reopening to a halt; As holidays approach, CDC urges Americans to stay home, limit the size of gatherings, and avoid people not in the same household

oooo0oooo

I stayed in Asheville for four months, grieving. Grieving or loving or being loved. Through August, September, October, and November. The three of us devoted to the unfurling Fern's face in the morning—smiling up from her crib. I watched Fern's powers grow: her hands becoming more deliberate, her legs stretching, urging to stand up. I watched and could not help mourning this too, as Fern separated herself from something bigger, becoming, for better or for worse, a world unto herself.

When school started again, the kids and teachers were still all at home because of concerns about the spread of the virus. Both Bryson and Justine went off to separate rooms to instruct a quilt of children's faces on their computer screens. Bryson tried to get his ninth graders to do home labs with household chemicals, and Justine negotiated orchestral themes with the high school string section sitting at their kitchen tables at home. I gladly took the morning shift with Fern, feeding her in a high chair, taking her for walks through the neighborhood. To be useful was curative; without it, I would have floundered even more. Whenever they could get a break, Justine and Bryson came to wherever we were in the house or in the backyard, swooping in to hold her, to the giggling delight of Fern.

Fern quickly lost her fear for me once I was no longer trapped behind glass, and once she trusted I could be counted on just like her parents. Fern sucked on her hands and still sometimes put those sticky hands in my mouth as if it were her own mouth. I fell in love with the soles of Fern's feet, their plump innocence not yet walked on. I would kiss them dutifully every morning before lifting her from her crib. Fern's legs pumped and it became a game that Fern slyly formulated herself. Both of us laughing: trying to keep her soles from being kissed, wanting her soles to be kissed.

Fern helped me to remember to laugh—helped expand my chest that felt stomped into submission upon Aakash's death.

Caring for Fern entered my dreams. Rather than Fern, though, I held Aakash: he became the infant I never had. I savored the feel of him in my arms: his warmth, his small, almost creaturely heft. I didn't want to put him down, and he didn't want to be put down. The recurring dream was always accompanied by a knocking at the door that turned into a mechanical sound as if the door were made of metal. Someone or something wanted the baby back, and I wept when I had to release him to the sound of the knocking. I often woke crying angrily in the humid dark, looking into the churning blades of the overhead fan.

In the evenings, after Justine or Bryson had put Fern down, we would gather on the back deck, looking into the deciduous woods as they began to yellow, then orange, then singe with deeper colors.

One evening, when I told Justine and Bryson about my Aakash dream, Justine suggested I change the scene myself.

I used to do it all the time; it's called lucid dreaming, Justine said, laughing and holding a goblet of dark wine. Her amber eyes always looked at me with such clarity. Justine was young enough, thirty-five, to be my own daughter. She and Bryson often teased me, calling me Fern's *white grandma.* Justine's self-assurance and belief in herself and her talent were so like Aakash's. I'd have been lucky to be her mother.

Yet, of course, Justine felt just as thrown by Aakash's death as I did. *It's like being bucked off a horse,* she said once. Yes, we'd been flipped off onto the ground of being, just these limited individuals. Once again, I was the solitary Z—feeling like just another ruined, aging human, wanting something back that wasn't ever mine to keep.

I used to make anything happen that I wanted in dreams! Until it came to getting all my dead people to come on out and play in my dreams, Justine said.

Bryson and I laughed. *What the living eff, Jus! All your dead people? Sounds like an unholy bargain to me,* Bryson said.

You know, I just couldn't get Marvin Gaye to come on in and sing with me, or Michael Jackson to come on in and dance with me, Justine said.

Your powers did not extend to dead celebrities or all dead people? I asked.

Well, I did so want to commune with my Aunt Bernice, and she never showed up either. Justine shook her head. We all sat looking into the trees, the silence lengthening as fireflies started to rise and infiltrate the dark.

On the other hand, Justine looked down into her wine, *maybe the dream is telling you that you just want to hold onto him a little longer, Z. Nothing wrong with that.* Her lips pressed together, and she set the glass down. *Aakash is there for you in your dreams at least,* Justine said.

She walked back into the house quietly. I knew that Justine's grief troubled her. She and Aakash had remained good friends. They called each other frequently and used to meet up at some of the same spiritual retreats across the southeast. Justine said that at silent retreats, she appreciated the way they could hold steady in each other's eyes. *I miss Aakash's smile too*, she'd said. *That boy could set you straight with his smile.*

You don't have to protect me from it—you know, your mourning, I said once, after Justine had left the room in just this way.

It's how I want to do it, she had said. *By myself.*

At first, I used to sit in an awkward silence with Bryson when Justine left. That's when I realized how inward Bryson was. But this quality, so unlike Aakash's, had a different kind of comfort in it. Bryson's silence often released me from thinking.

Lately though, he had become fascinated with learning more about Yellow. Had read everything he could.

Here's something I just learned, Bryson said. Two candles wavered on the table in front of him. *Fascinating stuff. When that researcher dude Nakagaki came up with the idea to have Physarum go through a maze? Heading toward a flake of oatmeal at the other end, Physarum always chooses the most direct route. It does not get caught in dead ends. It goes for the simplest and most direct way to feed itself. I mean it traced the Japanese subway system—tracking what urban planners had already determined was the most efficient system. What do you make of that? I mean, big picture?*

He tapped the table with his knuckle. Bryson had a science mind, but he did like to hear what Aakash and I had understood about Yellow.

Well—I investigated the rustling darkness—*don't you think we really exist in the same kind of maze—life? And that we think all choices exist and are open for us too? We keep trying to decide what's going to be best . . . will we second-guess ourselves all the time, will we take the long, complicated road? Will we resist what we hate and grasp for what we want? We are not Yellow that goes for the direct, least complicated route. Most of us, anyway.* I thought of my doomed love for Maude. Maude who made use of the faeries in the way she knew how—in a way that was just right for her—for wherever she was going. Eventually into that icy white penthouse apartment above New York City.

Bryson sat forward, pushing his glasses up on his nose, and took a swig from his beer bottle. Small animals scurried in the undergrowth.

I continued, thinking what Aakash would have added. *But Yellow knows—*

with all parts of themself, that not only are you on the path, but the direct path has been set in eternity. To not resist, to go where you are intuited to go, means that you are on the path. I drew air into my lungs, air that sometimes felt like glass these days.

He shook his head. *It's been set? And, uh . . . eternity? Don't get me wrong, but our intuitions are false all the time. I don't know if I buy that. Although,* he used a wet finger around his glass so that it rang at a high pitch, *There is something about it that rings inside me.*

I didn't say it's always the right path. We're just on it. I smiled at him, his face wavering in the candlelight.

I'm still trying to sit with the idea that Physarum has a consciousness. No offense, but you, Jus, and Aakash don't think like scientists. I'm still doing my research.

I liked how Bryson always put Aakash back in the present-tense.

Hey, I've been thinking . . . I watched as individual leaves flapped on the tree above me, like multiple hands waving from one great source. *Will you help me culture some?*

That's research, for sure, Bryson scratched his scalp, looking at me over the top of his glasses. *Hell, girl,* he said in a low voice. L*et's do it!* He nodded his head and rapped the table again. *This is what I like about science. The surprise! You never know how the story's going to end.*

Tears sprang into my eyes, and the moth that had been trapped for so long in my throat opened its wings. So maybe, just maybe, I could have this: seeing Yellow again. To be with Yellow. I smiled, touched his arched hand, then got up from the table and stood at the railing. The silence between us exactly right. I had resisted the wine every evening but not the smoke. I lit a joint and, as I puffed and let it out, heard the sliding glass door open. In one hand, Justine held a bowl of berries with whipped cream and in the other a bag of tortilla chips.

What's your pleasure? she asked, her eyes still tear-damp.

I pointed at the bag, Bryson the berries. *Then let's get at it.* She scudded out a chair and plopped down.

We're going to raise us up some Yellow, Bryson said, putting an arm around Justine, then lightly kissing her forehead. They gazed at each other, and I turned back to look into the woods as their heads bent together. *You right now?* I heard Bryson say. The throb of the tree frogs echoed Bryson's comfort.

Yeahhh, came Justine's reply, *I'm right. So Yellow then*? she said louder. *That's cool, that's cool.*

I reached into the chip bag, feeling lightly buoyed.

We're gonna do it, Bryson said, nodding his head. *And I want to see it. This Physarum shit keeps splitting its nuclei, but it's still just one cell. Even if I'm not onboard for all this consciousness stuff; this is going to be dope.* He lightly smacked the table.

For instance, he continued, *Physarum doesn't like salt, so its growth slows down when it gets a taste.*

You holding class now? Justine winked at me.

But, yeah, whatever—listen: this stuff will habituate to it. First, it moves slowly across the salt bridge; it's not so sure. But days later, it will cross the bridge at its normal rate. When it meets another brother—or yeah, yeah, sister—its instinct is to become one with it, and if a salt-eating Physarum meets one that hasn't eaten salt then the new one will acclimate and will like salt too.

It's like a trauma, Justine said. *Right? The salt? But we must bear with it. We must acclimate, like you say. Go over the damn bridge.*

And the next one, and the next one, I said, the crunch of the chips echoing in my ears.

Ugh. Now you're just talking in metaphors. But, okay, salt is the trauma? Bryson asked.

I sat down on the deck, looking at my thin bare feet, thinking of Clem walking on water as it rose. I was a little high, and it felt good.

You just said it. They take it slowly. The trauma becomes part of them, then part of any bigger Yellow, I said, remembering how Aakash and I had laughed in the dark together at Yellow's ways: they were so simple. *That's because Yellow is always awake, is always aware of something singular about us all. Trauma often moves us to go deeper, doesn't it?*

If we are in our best mind, like Aakash, then we actually like it, Justine said. *How many times has he told us that that whole bathtub phase arrived to save him?*

And to see ourselves in the source of trauma: whether it's an event or a person, I said, blinking. There was the bear, and there was Holiday. I let out a long sigh.

I don't understand, Bryson said.

I don't understand the man who molested me. Or our current president. Or the pandemic. But here I am. And it's for something, if we let that happen.

Trump is *our nation's trauma. No, actually*—Justine crunched the chips—*he's the fucking world's trauma.*

Don't get me started. Bryson held up the spoon and let a dollop of whipped cream sail off into the night. We heard it splatter against a tree. *Letting loose a little white stuff.*

Justine's laugh was infectious, and I stretched flat on the deck, the laughter rippling through my spine. Light pollution, even in Asheville, blocked most of the stars, yet somehow, I could still feel their presence.

Gimme some of that, Bryson said.

I passed the joint over to him.

Aakash says that we can't fight reality, just be awake to it, I said.

Be woke! Justine said.

Tough job, I replied.

For white people anyway, Justine laughed. *Catch up!*

Point taken, I said. *You know, for most of my life I heard what Yellow told me as, 'One side loves the other.' The night I saw the bear, I heard it right: 'One side loves the other as the other.'*

You heard . . . Yellow? Bryson leaned forward, the smoke curling into the darkness as he looked at me. He shook his head. *Good Lord.*

Come on, Bry, Justine said. *Catch up. Or, I mean, go with it. One side loves the other as the other. Or I am that.*

The evening was perfect. And imperfect. It was difficult without Aakash, who was no longer traveling in India. And it was easy.

Justine brought out her cello and played, her head tilted, the strength of her arm moving with the bow, her cheekbones catching the moonlight. There was the sound of Aakash in it, his story, but I didn't say anything because maybe there wasn't. Maybe it was a bigger story. Justine's story. Or even the magic bang.

oooo0oooo

That night as I carried Aakash in a soft blanket, the mechanical knocking began again. *It's no trouble, really no trouble at all*, I wanted to say. At least for me. The fear mounted because I knew I'd have to give him up as before. The small Aakash would shrink to nothing, and I would once again stand bereft, hearing the insistent knocking.

This time I looked at the baby Aakash and snuggled into his spicy scent. Could you close your eyes in a dream? No, I could not. Looking into his troubled eyes that were so like Fern's when she first saw me, I knew he wanted to be set down.

You've grown too big for me, I said. *I can't carry you anymore*. Then his eyes looked into mine, and I realized he was standing in front of me. The mechanical knocking of that monstrous machine—all there was to keep him breathing—turned into a hum, and then the hum became Justine's cello. Full-bodied, throbbing like blood.

I did that. I changed the music, I thought. But I couldn't change Aakash's leaving, and so, I imagined us both in India, a place I'd only heard about from him. I imagined the two of us together in some hot tropical landscape, and this time when I turned to him, he was Aakash with his small graying goatee and his blinding white teeth. His breath was a blinding white light too, and I leaned my forehead into his and felt the slight give, like a body coming apart, and then I was through him, and I fell into weightless stars. Everywhere.

oooo0oooo

MATERIALS:

plate culture of Physarum polycephalum (plasmodium)	1
box of five Physarum sclerotia	1
bottle of sterile 2% agar	4
package of oat flakes	2
sterile petri dishes	20
disposable sterile scalpel	5
autoclave bag with twist tie	1
sterile water (rehydration medium)	1
Digital Resource Instruction card	1
Teacher's Manual	1

A week before Halloween, we cultured Yellow in the twenty agar plates provided by the mail-in science kit I ordered. Together we stood in Bryson's high school bio classroom on a Saturday among the long gray tables outfitted with Bunsen burners and small sinks. No one had entered the lab since the previous March.

Dude. Why'd you get the kit with the agar plates? I've got plenty of plates and agar here in the lab, he said.

Would you have to pay for them? I asked. He nodded. *Well, yeah, okay. There are tons just sitting around unused, but I'm an ethical guy.*

That's why I got them, I said.

He stacked the plates, both of us masked and gloved. He looked down at me, his glasses sliding down, but he didn't touch his glasses with his gloved hand. I'd already gotten a lesson about maintaining a sterile environment.

I get why people are freaked out now. If you're in the sciences, you're not freaked out. People are suddenly: oh my god! Bacteria is floating everywhere. Damn straight bacteria and viruses are floating everywhere. It just took a pandemic for the rest of you to realize it.

With precision, he walked me through the steps to place the plasmodium on each plate. He watched with weariness as I waved the lit tweezers in the air after flaming it over the Bunsen burner.

Remember? he prompted.

Oh yeah, I said. *Everything's contaminated.*

Welcome to the real world, he said. I used tweezers to put five oat flakes on top of the agar. The plasmodium sat directly at the center. That little immortality, waiting.

We worked side by side, the entire building silent.

We're doing science, he said a half hour in, his voice rising. *I fucking love science!*

Why? I asked. To me, the vision of Yellow at the center of each plate felt like possibility, felt like wonder.

For one, there's a certain kind of quiet. We don't have to talk. It's all about the elements—you know, the basics. And, of course, not knowing the ending.

Not knowing the ending lit in my mind like the Bunsen flame—a flare he threw out ahead of us.

I feel the same way, I said.

Back at the carriage house, each day I took out the covered trays from the cabinet and marveled at their growth. Yellow sent out lace-like tendrils to overtake each oat. I thought of them as newborns with bolts of energy under their feet—or pseudopods, technically. Their very existence was a kind of arousal, like vibrations that could pass through me.

Every day, I tracked their growth as they branched out to the far reaches of the dishes. We had bagged each dish, and the yellow tendrils crawled right out of the dishes and into the bags.

Getting them beyond the bags took more work and research on Bryson's part, yet soon he got them settled in a tub on a decaying log. We had to keep the log darkened, wet, and humid.

We plated more of Yellow just in case, and on the day I left, these sat in a dark satchel in the passenger seat of the Karmann Ghia nestled close to the sealed tub with the log now covered with oats, mushrooms, and the finely textured Yellow.

Before I drove away from Asheville, we all huddled together standing on the front driveway. Since Aakash's death, crying about anything and everything was no longer a problem for me or Justine. She'd learned to come out of hiding and into my arms. But upsetting Fern on this last day wasn't what we wanted. So we clamped our lips tight and all stood in a tight rose formation with Fern at the center. Because it must have seemed to her like an impossibly funny closeness, Fern's laughter bubbled over like the trilling of a bird. I drove away thinking of Fern's bright face at the center of our circle. Now I'd be left with my only progeny: Yellow.

oooOoooo

It was the day before Thanksgiving that I left my new family behind. Though the CDC discouraged all gatherings, even among families, Frank had called and invited me to join them on my way back to the Quarter. Said he didn't care because he didn't believe in COVID-19 anyway. In a halting, embarrassed way, he told me he was sorry to hear about Aakash, was glad to have met him. A huge contradiction since Aakash had died of COVID-19, but I listened as he cleared his throat.

Seemed like one in a million, that guy, he muttered. So, on my way back home to New Orleans, I stopped at Frank's near Shreveport. *Out in the sticks*, he liked to say. After dinner, we all walked in the woods, making our way past the trash cars. The trees were stark now, and Frank's wife and kids walked ahead of the two of us. The older two boys were in their twenties now, hair shaved close. Both worked for Frank's construction outfit. One was just married; his pregnant wife wore an oversized flannel shirt. The boys walked together, hands in pockets, and the new bride walked with Frank's wife. The younger pre-teen girls shared one cell phone between them, tucked into Gracie's rear right pocket. Each one wore an AirPod like a dangling bone earring.

As Frank and I crunched through the spent leaves, he asked the unexpected: *You think Clem and I would still look identical if he was alive?* I stopped, looking at Frank closely. He had worn his hair in a buzz cut since high school, so unlike Clem's golden locs. Now, at fifty-two, he'd lost most of his hair, just like our father. He'd always been heavier than Clem and moved with dragging feet rather than Clem's smooth lope. By the time they were teenagers, everyone knew who was who. But I kept all these facts to myself. I also didn't say the obvious: Clem was one in a million too. The apricot sunset behind Frank warmed his features, and in the blue eyes looking down at me that had suddenly gone tender, I could see that, of course, they were the same.

I think it'd be hard to tell you two apart, I said. Frank reached out and grabbed my forearms, as if I'd saved him from something. I pulled him close.

oooo0oooo

On Christmas Day, I rode the streetcar with Aakash's camera on my lap. One thing I loved most about riding the streetcars was the sounds of their efforts. The electric glide along the track, the rhythmic throb of the wheels, a periodic clanking of the bell, the mechanical wheeze of the brakes bringing the car to a stop. The effort—all these hard and fast illusions—were part of reliving the memory. Aakash and I had done just this every Christmas Day. We rode the streetcar lines intuitively. Sometimes we'd ride to City Park, where we would wander past the museum, sometimes to Audubon Park, and sometimes to the soul-veg place in Tremé. Today, I wanted to be pushed and pulled helplessly by the streetcar and sat near the front, taking the St. Charles route through the Garden District with no set destination in mind.

At home, in Aakash's old darkroom, where I'd set up Yellow under what Bryson had specified were just the right kind of heat lamps, they surrendered in just the same way. I imagined Aakash saying that where they would go and how they would go had been written long ago. Like the branching interlacing pulse of the slime mold, I was also an organism, so to speak, but also just vibration—or so the physicists say—being pushed and pulled by a force that had always gently throbbed within me. It throbbed even at twelve, as I knelt over Yellow in my Metairie backyard marveling at their growth, or threw plums at their accepting mass, or wept for their loss.

The streetcar's driver was named Peach. The joyful expression in her eyes told me that she was grinning under her mask when I got on at Canal Street. She'd been our driver more than once on Christmas Day. Her grin said she recognized me from some year past. But minus whom, she didn't quite remember. This saved me any explanation.

The route of the streetcar curved and branched so that the passengers' bodies, standing or sitting, often shifted and jostled. The standing bodies swayed as they held on to the leather straps and the seated bodies bumped shoulders. That was another thing I loved about the ride. It rendered us all so material—

thrown by forces we could not control. And yet immaterial—just beauties on the planet. Though who among us recognized that fact?

The interior of the streetcar was also beautiful: the curved dome of the yellowed ceiling, the brass fittings, the mahogany seats that moved to face the front or to fold out so that passengers could face each other. The capsule of the car glowed as light sifted in from the side windows, forcing passengers to squint. The passengers held poses of expectation—*Should they get off at this stop*?—or they had quiet exteriors while their interior minds churned. The effort of their thinking showed on their faces. Or sometimes, they appeared as the children did—drawn into the rush, a sheer and contagious excitement at being on such a wild ride. I observed myself being drawn to each of these reactions—my mind looping on memories with Aakash and his almost vivid embodiment next to me on the seat. How if I looked a little to the left, I might see the brown depths of his eyes looking back at me. I'd never met anyone else who could look so deeply into each person he met.

The ride became a meditation, with the chill air coming in through the half-opened windows and the shifting presence of the bodies wrapped tightly in wool or synthetic coats and hats—Everyone masked—beneath all that, the feeling of all of them as a mass streaming forward. I felt an awareness underneath it all: glowing and throbbing just as Yellow incrementally took over the log.

The presence of the digital camera on my lap was not to capture the sights; I brought it to finally look at the images Aakash had taken in India. I suppose I'd made a thing of it. Something Aakash would say when I set up my *little altars* as he called them, where I propped postcards, ticket stubs, and museum guides from our most recent vacation. *Are you making it a ceremony thing?* he would ask.

Yes, I often said back. This ceremony felt active enough to insulate me from the impact of his physical absence from my life, from this holiday, and from the empty wooden seat next to me. And maybe a technique to maintain my composure amid strangers as I looked at his last days before he found himself in the hospital with COVID-19.

How I got the camera was another kind of passage. I had talked to Aakash's mother, Astha, on the phone when I was still in Asheville. Talking wasn't quite the word; instead, exchanging condolences and quietly crying was more how it went. Yet from what I knew, Astha only thought of me as her son's roommate and good friend. Aakash didn't regularly share with anyone in his family where we went or what we did together. When Astha called me from

Virginia saying that she had received Aakash's personal effects from India, I noticed a slight change in her tone. Puzzled? Softer?

Do you have the password for Aakash's phone? Astha asked me.

No, I don't. But since Aakash and I had shared the same cell service in our names, I trusted that if the phone were returned, I might be able to unlock it. Astha also had his digital camera. She and Aakash's father had looked at the images and printed many of them out.

So lovely. How he captured India was like he had taken snapshots of my childhood, Astha said.

That must be so incredible, I said.

Oh, it is not incredible. That is who Aakash was.

Aakash in the past tense always landed in my throat. That moth trapped and fluttering for freedom.

Z—Astha's pronunciation of *Zee* came out in a long sibilance between her teeth, as if almost reverently spoken. *We have determined that the phone and the camera belong to you. I will send you both straightaway.*

I was left wondering what they had found on the camera. How far back did the digital disk go?

The streetcar went around Lee Circle, the statue of Robert E. Lee thankfully taken down in 2017. I remembered being next to the window one Christmas, and as the car took the circular turn, my body leaned into Aakash's. Rather than relax into the turn as I had, he held his spine straight so that my body was a kind of collapse against his. He had always been so solid, so unlike my fragmented mother who doled out love when it occurred to her. And not like my father either, whose resentment remained diffuse, leftover from who knows what. These bodies are figments, Aakash would say, and yet I'd mistaken him for permanence, for a forever.

When I opened the box from Astha a few days before, there was more than just his iPhone and the camera. Inside was his wallet and a sealed envelope with my name written in purple ink. I could not resist opening his striped fabric wallet first because I remembered his habit of tucking a sticky pad inside where he jotted notes to himself. I would come across so many of these that I'd finally decided he needed a drawer in his room to keep them in. Among the folded rupees, I found it. The plain yellow pad with the corners creased up as if taking flight. An origami swan. The notes were a small, abbreviated diary of his journey—beginning with his aunt and uncle's contact information, then notes for his railway travels—times and destinations. He'd jotted down names of restaurants in various cities. Then the note reading *Pramod* with a phone number. Beneath that *Rajasthan*, *CRATER* underlined, and *world's navel*. Then the final note: *Tell Z about panspermia*.

But he didn't tell me; he didn't call. I flung the sticky pad down on the table.

Panpsychic, the wood sprite had told me last summer, maybe the same day that a man named Pramod had told Aakash about panspermia. The all? One about the mind and one about the body?

The note from Astha I didn't open. I had waited until today before I looked at the images on his camera.

Past Lee Circle, the streetcar went along on St. Charles Street, the block now shorn of many of the live oaks since Hurricane Katrina came through. The beautiful southern houses in the Garden District stood like sentinels, observers of my past and my present.

You ***are*** *making a ceremony of it*, Aakash would say, head shaking. I sighed and the Asian toddler sitting in the seat in front of me turned to look, her unmasked face smiling. I mimed a smile with my fingers over my own mask, and the girl looked back to her mother, giggling.

I opened the envelope and then abruptly decided to look at the images first.

Goats running along the side of the road. Several shots that looked as if they were just outside the window of a van. Aakash's best photo in the stream was of a young girl in a seat in front of him. How interesting these resemblances. Her small finger touched the window and her face in profile smiled broadly. The goats beneath the window were caught in the light's shimmer. It was as if the same little girl kept turning to look fully into my eyes. But there were no goats hurrying alongside the streetcars of New Orleans.

Aakash's travels unfolded in reverse as I pressed the back button: two little girls chased each other around the carved pillars of a sandstone-colored temple. Their motion captured in a long exposure so that they had become see-through.

I kept going backwards, just as Aakash's parents must have done, until I reached the image of his shopworn aunt and uncle standing in the bustling airport of Mumbai, their faces streaked with shadows.

The streetcar lunged to a stop. Peach said Merry Christmas to the tourists who hopped down the steps to City Park. I waved to the toddler who snuck a shy peek around her mother's leg as they stepped off the car. Peach stood. Seeing that I remained, she pointed and inclined her head to the accordion-folded door: an open question.

Is this car going back? I asked, raising my voice to get past the mask. Peach gave a thumbs-up, so I signaled the same back. Peach nodded and got off to shift the railway tracks. After reversing the wooden seat back to face towards home, I looked down at the next image—which turned out to be the last—and yet really, the first.

Our last morning together. I was sleeping naked, entwined in our golden comforter so that only the hillock of my left hip showed and my right breast. Aakash's forearm extended into the frame—dark and beautiful. Had he positioned it to look so like the silhouette I had made of his forearm and hand so many years ago? When something about the possibility of his touch had aroused me? But not just his touch, his very being?

Of course. He was reaching towards me so that the scar showed and as if the bliss of my sleep could not be awakened. The golden drape of the comforter as well as the way morning light had angled through the balcony windows and pooled along the ridges of my body seemed like a kind of awareness. He had made this image and didn't erase it. And because I had made a ceremony of the discovery, it felt as though Aakash had been riding alongside me all the time.

I thought of Yellow enveloping me, like the golden comforter in the photo. Could it be a performance and a kind of meditation? The very thought—the art of it and the reality of it—had been in my peripheral vision for some time.

I pulled out Astha's note from the unsealed envelope.

> Z—
> Our dear son's personal effects we here return to you, daughter-in-law.

I looked up. New passengers boarded at each end of the car; even behind their masks, they talked with excited voices, shuffling to find their seats. I gulped air under the mask. Briefly closed my eyes. *Daughter-in-law.*

> In due time, we will sort out Aakash's finances so that you have no worries.
> We welcome you to the family—as you have always been welcome. Do what you think best with his photographs that are so dear to us. And please, come visit.
> Your parents, Astha & Sharma

My parents. I put my head in my lap, my body rocking, feeling as the car rumbled to a start on its journey that the wheels beneath me sparked along the tracks, and the humming of the streetcar could also be the hum of Yellow traversing the city.

Yellow was almost animal, almost plant. The bolts that moved them were the energy of a cosmos. Yellow massed, masses plumed, and spiraled across the planet. Light had feet; light had wings.

oooo0oooo

Pandemic Timeline

December 2020: FDA grants Pfizer-BioNTech first Emergency Use Authorization (EUA) for an mRNA vaccine, a new type of vaccine that has proven to be highly effective against COVID-19; A week later, EUA granted to Moderna, also for an mRNA vaccine Vaccinations begin; however, major variants of the virus also circulate The UK reports a new variant of the virus, B.1.1.7, could be more contagious; By the end of the month, B.1.1.7 is detected in the US

January 2021: In the US, the number of cases and deaths begin to fall; More variants spread; Around the world, efforts escalate to vaccinate as many people as possible to slow the variants' spread Researchers work to understand how deadly or contagious variants are compared to the original virus

February 2021: Demand for the vaccine exceeds supply; Biden Administration expects the addition of a third Johnson & Johnson alternative to make vaccines more available; Companies work to tweak products to make distribution easier and to control new variants

More than one hundred million people around the world have been infected by COVID-19 and more than 2.5 million people have died of the disease

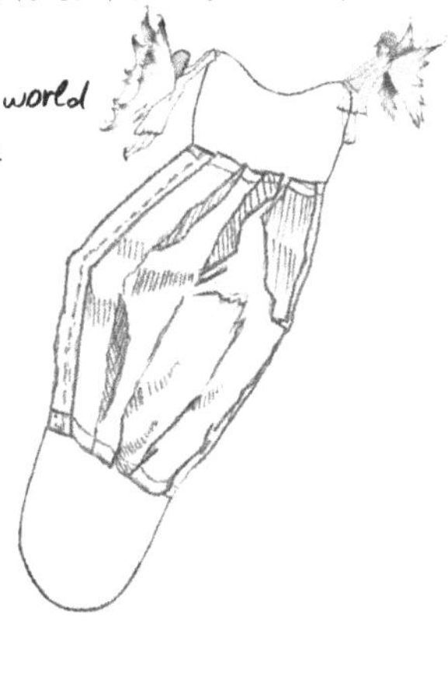

oooоOoooo

There was so much I wanted to tell Aakash now:

- that if only I could come across his sticky note fragments—all that reaching after the ethereal—how I longed to see his thickly curled handwriting again. Why did I insist on a drawer when the sticky notes were an art as well?
- that being with him and watching his easy nature with everyone he met inspired me to be better, to look further into all the lives around me.
- that his careful listening mattered. That his small humorous gestures—like bringing home one ripe avocado and setting it in the center of a platter wearing a cap as a top hat made me laugh. So many laughs that were ours.
- that he was right: we should have looked for the street artist Odessa and asked her what else she knew about extraterrestrial life.
- that his photographs glimmer with the edges of the unseen, but I told him that, hadn't I? Hadn't I?
- that after our third year together, I knew he loved me as much as he had loved Anjali. That we were one and the same.
- that I finally came to understand Holiday, had seen the transparency of him. Had put him in his grave.
- that he helped me to recover myself.

oooоOoooo

Local Artist in One-Woman Plus One-Organism Show

At the intersection of art and science, local artist Z Knotts will debut her most recent installation at the NOLA Historic Lofts for three days, March 12 to 14, marking the one-year anniversary of the pandemic.

The socially distanced and masked event titled *Yellow* will feature Ms. Knotts with her primary working material, what she calls an "always advancing, ever knowing" slime mold that has taken the scientific community by storm. Named *Physarum polycephalum*, the mold is a one-celled organism containing many nuclei, an anomaly in plant and animal life. Experiments have shown that it can find the most direct route through a maze, has 720 sexes, and is immortal, meaning it will turn to dust but can regenerate. Knotts remarks that "some say that the *Physarum's* way of being can show us that consciousness is not limited to the human brain. I think that Yellow teaches us that consciousness is everywhere; we are just one of the many vessels for it."

Knotts says her goal is to spark conversation on ideas of suffering, community, and life and death itself: "The Black Lives Matter movement has shown us that people want true social justice; they want societies free of nationalism and racism, and the pandemic has shown us that people also want personal meaning, an understanding beyond our individual selves." She adds, however, that it is not for her to interpret her art, rather for her viewers to respond to the slime mold's art-making for themselves.

"If you just want to observe Yellow's growth, then the show is for that too. The branching and fractal patterns of the *Physarum* are beautiful in and of themselves. It's awe-inspiring just to see how the mold grows, advances, and looks for themself to be with themself."

Knotts' works have typically integrated other media. Her *Tales from the Flood* made use of news footage and personal interviews and put the audience in a simulated "eye of Hurricane Katrina" with an LCD projection, while also demonstrating the chaos of NOLA's tragedy, especially for the city's homeless population. Earlier works have explored the impact of childhood molestation, and her custom wall art incorporates how we imbue our everyday objects with an "almost uncanny intelligence."

Knotts' fascination with the *Physarum* began when she was a young girl after her mother discovered the organism in their backyard and brought it to the attention of LSU's Biology lab. She says: "If my mother hadn't alerted the scientific institutions by providing them with the specimen from our backyard, perhaps our scientists would not have learned as much as we now know. Yellow could have come from an asteroid 100 million years ago and has always been here, or maybe it came back on a spacecraft during one of NASA's many interstellar space missions. We don't know, but it can teach us valuable lessons not just about consciousness, but the nature of the material world."

The exhibit will be accompanied by the recorded music of award-winning composer and cellist Justine Adams. Her partner, Bryson Adams, is a biologist, and according to Knotts, he "designed the perfect environment where Yellow can flourish."

Parental advisories are in place for some nudity. The darkened gallery space is limited to six masked viewers at a time. Tickets are encouraged. Follow the link for this limited engagement show.

oooo0oooo

Developments in technology may eventually help security experts restore the missing audio on the Watergate tape. Owned by the National Archives and Records Administration, of the tape, a recording the eighteen and a half minutes of the meeting between President Nixon (d. April 22, 1994) and his Chief of Staff, H. R. Haldeman (d. November 12, 1993) remains unintelligible.

Efforts have been made to reconstruct the meeting using Haldeman's handwritten notes, but that attempt has failed. Now in a climate-controlled vault, the tape awaits the future when technology will bring us new discoveries.

oooоOoooo

We came to the gallery at the tail end of the long winter, when the surges of infection came in waves across the country. We had been afraid, or we had been alone, or we had been sick, or we had survived.

Or we had lost people we had loved. Parents, grandparents, friends, neighbors as well as doctors, nurses, the people who had tried to save us. The quiet, the generous, the robust, the beautiful ones. Those you may not notice. But we noticed. We had lost jobs, we had lost our housing, we had part-time jobs as *essential workers.* We tried to make ends meet. We had loss—we were loss.

Businesses shuttered; people scattered. At the edges of town, lines of cars still circled the drive-thru COVID-19 testing centers.

We were still reeling after the tumultuous start of the year. We were still a country divided. We had existed in alternate worlds; we did not know yet where those worlds would meet. We held a suffused anger, or we were beginning to feel relief.

We were ready for something new; we were ready to leave our houses—our computers and phones lit with the worlds we'd immersed ourselves in. The year had worn at us; for some, the year had awakened us.

Some of us were vaccinated, more of us would be. Some refused.

We had no expectations. We had so many expectations. For sensation? For truth? We did not know.

We didn't bring our children. Some, the ones that had lived here a long time, brought their children. Nudity? It was New Orleans.

Or we knew her, from when we were children. Ms. Knotts. Z. Quiet, small, at any moment she might take flight. But even when her hands weren't cradling what we made, we felt she held us. That everything we touched could be art.

Or she was a stranger to us.

We were interested in the word *Yellow,* interested in what it could mean spelled out on the gallery door in tendrils, like something reaching for us. We didn't know why we wanted to go; it was so unexpected, but there it was. The word *Yellow*.

We came in alone, or in twos, sometimes threes. Sometimes a family. We walked into the dimly lit anteroom wearing our masks. We were told it would be safe. There would be no interaction with the artist. Nothing to touch. Only six people at a time for the viewing, or a family of up to ten. We were given a time limit of twenty minutes per group. Some laughed nervously, making the odd joke. Most were silent.

We walked through another door and down a corridor we couldn't really see. A trail of lights on the floor directed us, as if through a tunnel—then the open space of sound. The tinkling of wind chimes reminded us of dusk deepening into evening.

We heard birds settling into trees, their last calls to each other. We heard their wings flying close to our heads. We remembered our times in the woods, in the bayous, near the gulf or the ocean. We remembered those times when nature brought us closer, closer to something beating.

At the edges of the room, we saw the small tent-like structures that held wavering lights—like candles in a forest. Along the walls, the majestic outlines of huge trees like sequoias reaching towards clouds.

We saw, just ahead, what looked like a glass box, a see-through coffin, a terrarium lit from below.

As we got closer, the sound of a cello, slow and as if rising in our blood.

Incredibly, walking towards it in the dim light, we saw the woman in the box. We saw her body pale against the thick moss, the mud-colored leaves, a tree stump twisted next to her as she was twisted, one arm raised. Her eyes were closed. No, her eyes were open.

Her hair spread around her in long silver rivulets, like water traveling along the forest floor. Did we hear the sound of water? We couldn't be sure.

She was covered, we could see, only by the thinnest layer of leaves and loose soil, but clearer against that darkened shadow were the spreading veins of what must be the slime mold. Over her feet like yellow lace and in other places thick as ropes that spread into tangled knots across her stomach, across her breasts. In the palms of her hands and all around the edges of her body, the slime mold was puffed and thick, blobs of what we realized was the material she wanted us to see—Yellow. The lights under her body changed so that her skin looked dappled green and brown as the forest floor. On screens above her, we could see the time-lapsed stills of Yellow moving—splices of how Yellow was at first just branching across her skin, then Yellow gathered substance and form, heading towards the flakes of oats, centered on her belly or in her hands. The scenes brought us closer to its pulsing from the inside: how it all gathered with no sense of separation.

The music lifted—a light melody on piano keys, and then the cello was joined by violins, soaring incrementally as the projections did along the walls around the glass box. No longer were we among trees. Instead, the trees had shifted to veils of fireflies and the fireflies to stars. We'd thought of her in a terrarium, but as the lights beneath her changed, her skin took on the deep blue of space. Lights swirled around her. She was becoming one of the stars—Yellow all the time throbbing across her—their shape finding her shape. We were in echoless space, the sound of transmissions from a craft we couldn't see, and the glass box appeared to lift like a spaceship, celestial.

Her body never moved, and Yellow—thick or thin, lightly etched or her anchor—didn't seem to move either. Or were they moving together? Or was she? Was the sound coming from beyond us in the room or was the sound coming from the glass box?

Was the movement of their branching something we could see, advancing towards the material world or was everything always so still? Was she old or was she young? Was she speaking to us or was Yellow?

We would never be sure.

oooo0oooo

When Childress said I was brave, I didn't know what he meant and didn't dwell on it. *Everything is as it should be*, is what I said. Grizzled now, his freckles faded and his eyes searching mine, he had finally become himself. He handled everything I didn't want to handle: finding the space, setting up the marketing and ticketing, helping me to create the ideal conditions in the warehouse space for Yellow, and understood more of what I didn't even know I needed.

By the time of the show, I'd cut down on what I ate and what I drank, or maybe I was no longer hungry or thirsty; the important thing was that Yellow would be.

From eight different sites in the glass box, Bryson set Yellow to roam towards the oats spread across my body.

I meditated longer and longer in the months before the show, remembering how Aakash would sometimes be in his room an entire day. Could I do that? Yes.

Could I be the woman not frozen in ice, but a woman immersed in Yellow, a breathing woman for three days letting Yellow crawl across me? Yes.

Without Justine's music, could I have stayed in the reverie? No. And without Bryson's glass box, outfitted for everything, providing the perfect conditions for both me and Yellow to exist, it would not have become what I dreamed. And without those months caring for Fern with her parents and watching her existence becoming actual, could I have been restored after Aakash's death? No.

Could I have come to be what we've been dreaming all along—1 + 1 = 1?

oooo0oooo

There are times my body's so light I forget my body. Times it is my anchor. Times when every part of me wants to break open and be out of the box. To scream and to cry. But I let it pass. Try to inhabit, as well as I can, each moment in which everything passes: thirst, hunger, exhaustion. I sleep a few hours at night. Drink then. Am fed a little on breaks.

If I can turn without disturbing Yellow, Childress helps me.

I try to feel in those moments Yellow on me—their enveloping thought.

Once, opening my eyes, I see a man wearing his hygienic mask some fifty feet away, across the warehouse space. But also looking as if poised on the leaf nearest me, as if he were a man on a mountain.

Oh, my father, I think, though he never became real as a father to me. I let the thought pass. When he moves closer, I see it is Frank. He has come alone, and he smiles at me.

Another time, I feel like my mother stands in another corner of the room, unmasked, and I smell her quiet depression, like magnolia blooms with their browned creases. Her love is light and desperate.

I silently thank her and my father. Most of the time, they hadn't a clue—but they were part of my will as I was theirs. They burn like candles at the far edges of the room.

And Holiday. Something in me knows he has already died. I never did return to Lake Pontchartrain. Why would I? After Aakash's death, memory, like my body, only weighed me down. Why go again and again to the ways we are broken? Holiday broke me open. And for that, he came when he was meant to. *Thank you*. My lips form the words. Would I have fought so hard to make my life an art if he hadn't been part of my story?

Images of all the beings float and wrinkle: I remember the first time Aakash spoke to me at the residency.

Your name is very distinctive, he said. His eyes so darkly intense, I glanced away.

What do you mean? I asked.

Z Knotts is like Z Knows—that silent k. I looked at him in confusion. *At least it's the first word with a silent* k *that comes to mind.* His eyes danced.

But I didn't know anything, and I'd always thought my life was in knots. My name seemed a curse until he made my name a possibility. All my failures are why I'm here now is what I know. Late one day, through some mist, I see Astha, Sharma, and Aakash's sister Sharaya materialize and advance towards me in the box. I knew they would come because we spoke of it. Aakash's family that has become mine. Is it a mistake of my tired eyes that they look light-filled, almost glowing? Astha's fingers lightly touch the glass near my face. And as their eyes travel across Yellow's form, I see their wonder.

I didn't know anything when I first found Yellow; I was innocent of their advancing form. As Clem was too, as Clem and I had seen beings no one else could see, as Clem could float across the nation on trains going anywhere, as Clem could be weightless. He wanted, perhaps, to be swept up in the waters of Katrina. As Clem could gather jaguars and all the other beasts of his mental menagerie, poised with his majestic pinecone staff. Royalty of the air. What I thought had been a terrible curse did not mar Clem's life. He even told me so, but our lives and our actions unwound and blossomed as they should have.

I think of Maude—thief or warrior? A warrior thief, blameless and beautiful, weary and wary. Sending my faeries out to become the scintillating icons of New Orleans, doing what I couldn't do and doing it better. Casting her spells on me and me casting them back.

Because I had cast spells. Had hurt people like Jilly and a few others I had betrayed. I may have hurt others that I'd never know about.

Childress, somehow, once my mortal enemy, now my closest friend. The same—enemy-friend. A man who hurt enough he would not hurt others. *I told you your time would come*, he said. Maybe he did, and maybe he didn't.

Justine: my wise daughter, who took me in, her feet-on-the-ground husband, and Fern, the marvelous being they created. Just as beautiful as Newell. Brilliant creators and creations.

Then, finally, Aakash, again.

Here's the feeling—you are on me, in me, enveloping, creating. If that's not your voice in my head then it's my voice in my head, guiding Yellow's movements, or Yellow's guiding mine.

• • •

I open my eyes. Past the viewers looking, a blinking spatter of starlight—did I do that too? Did I create a dimension of stars or fireflies to peer into? Or Aakash?

Or Yellow, did you?

oooOoooo

If there were moonlight, could I love you any better?

Yes, and no, you say.

You need a surface more than me, better than me, I think.

Better, worse? These are ideas. I laugh without making a sound.

I feel the eros of one body on another. You on me. Finding your way to yourself. Striving for. Enveloping.

But no, you say. *No more striving. Better than eros.*

Time in which I let the words fill my cells, in which I empty my mind. And yet, the people come close, some tap on the glass. Clouds of their thoughts—their faces like balloons bobbing near me.

I feel like I can hear them, their ideas—when they get close to the glass, their mouths are silenced by their masks, by the quiet woods we have created. But the voices in their heads.

You do hear them, you say.

I hear their confusion.

You hear their confusion.

Grabbing onto anything they can.

Let go, you say.

Yes.

Go beyond their minds—dark or light clouds—go out into clouds.

Yes. Am I meeting you there? I ask.

You're always meeting me. As I am always meeting myself.

That makes me sad with joy.

Observe your sadness.

I feel it under my tongue. It can be erotic and true.

Yes, but what is a tongue? What is true? Beyond the clouds.

Beyond the clouds? I ask.

Five layers—you've named them.

I have?

First, the troposphere, the stratosphere, the mesosphere, then the thermosphere.

How long?

The longest—through the thermosphere—120 kilometers—next, the exosphere.

The exosphere . . . I can feel that. A heaviness.

The last of the gravitational pull.

The last?

Your density is so low that molecules are collisionless. You're in the uppermost layer of Earth time.

Earth time. Pete . . .

Yes, something he knew. Time itself brings us back to timelessness.

In the exosphere?

In the exosphere. No fear, above nor below.

No fear . . . I remember Duc's face undisturbed by the flames—a stillness so complete. In the exosphere, so little to pull him back to Earth. Virtually nothing.

And then?

Outer space. Inner space. These are all concepts so that you can know: anything that is infinite is indivisible.

Like you. And Aakash?

Indivisible.

Why couldn't I hear you all the time?

Life is a forgetting.

And remembering?

Yes. Sometimes, just at the last.

Through the exosphere?

Into the infinite.

ooooOoooo

I was one, and I was like many river stones for miles.

River water above, lapping the banks, the sun warming the river and the stones under the water.

I was one light; I was many. Like the fireflies you step into.

One dimension, two dimensions, three dimensions, four dimensions, five. The sixth. And more. More real than this real.

Fireflies lifting. You turn into them; you are them.

I wasn't your body; I was a body. Where you were, I was on you. Where you were, I was in you. Where you were, we were. Where you embraced, we embraced. If we were divided, we were whole.

The stream that meets, that braids. A stream as in your hair, as in your lashes, as in every follicle on your body. As in a touch across your body.

Where there was touch, there was no touch. Along the fallen log, along the branches, along then, your skin. Your skin, my skin.

We streamed into your hair. Into the leaves of your hair. Into the bark of your skin.

Into the bones. What bones? What time? What laughter? What weeping?

Every eye sees what it wants to see. Every scene is a play of forms. I overtake; you overtake.

Our dance, a thing of beauty. Suffused with all hands, all beauties. All beauties.

oooоOoooo

Interviewer: *What was the greatest challenge for you over your space career?*

Astronaut K: *Getting that solar panel up.*

[Looking into the camera, then beyond the camera. A look still enough to be anywhere.]

Can't think of anything wise or funny to say . . . Pete would though. He would.

Epilogue

In the eternity of continuous moments, the winged beings lift—gravity cannot hold them. Amid the solid answer to love, there is no answer.

In the eternity of the continuous present, Pete stands on the moon, watching planet Earth brim the horizon a marvelous ocean blue. Climates swarm over the marbled landforms where, invisible to the eye, Yellow goes to what nourishes them, as we all go—anchored by a consciousness both sacred and profane.

Did we go to the moon just to behold ourselves? The moon's lonely, pocked surface: *Sea of Crises, Sea of Vapors, Ocean of Storms, Sea of Fertility, Sea of Cold, Sea of Serenity, Sea that has Become Known*, and the one briefly misidentified as a sea, but no longer recognized: *Sea of Dreams.*

Peopled and elemental, Earth beholds the moon, showing its one face to us.

We never see it turn: the time taken to complete a rotation is the same time needed to complete an orbit around Earth.

Time's properties, human-made and illusory, split our infinity.

So you look at me and I look at you, and we behold each other, forever.

Notes

Portions of the original news item on Yellow are quoted from the May 31, 1973 issue of *The New York Times*, "Texas Scientists Think Backyard Blob Is Dead."

Details of Pete Conrad's life are compiled from his *The New York Times* obituary, various YouTube videos, and the book *Rocketman* by Nancy Conrad and Howard A. Klausner, New American Library, 2005.

Details about Conrad's sighting on Gemini 11 are from *The Strangest Encounters in Space: NASA's Unexplained Files* and Bruce Maccabee's reports on his website: *https://web.archive.org/web/20081108050107/http://brumac.8k.com/*

Skylab astronaut quotes are from *Skylab Space Station 1970s, NASA Documentary Film First American Space Station 67134*, PeriscopeFilm.

Details about Skylab are from *Saving Skylab: America's First Space Station*, Matt Alsup and Wes Pellerin, Directors, released April 18, 2020.

Details about Einstein are from *Rocketman*, *Encyclopedia Britannica*, the articles "Quantum-theory wars" by Ramin Skibba in *Nature*, "Einstein's Lonely Path" by Lee Smolin in *Discover*, and "When Einstein Met Tagore: A Remarkable Meeting of Minds on the Edge of Science and Spirituality" by Maria Popova on *The Marginalian*.

Rabindranath Tagore's lines were excerpted from his book of prose poems, *Gitanjali.*

Amended Interview with Astronaut Dr. Joseph P. Kerwin, NASA Johnson Space Center Oral History Project, Interviewed by Kevin M. Rusnak, Houston, Texas, May 12, 2000.

Timelines for 1973 and Hurricane Katrina adapted from Wikipedia.

Timelines for COVID-19 are from "Our Pandemic Year—A COVID-19 Timeline," *Yale Medicine* by Kathy Katella, March 9, 2021, with changes; Additionally, from the "CDC Museum COVID-19 Timeline": https://www.cdc.gov/museum/timeline/covid19.html

Aakash finds details on Khajuraho architecture from *The Hindu Temple* by Stella Kramrisch, 1976.

Bryson finds facts about *Physarum polycephalum* in the *NOVA* special, "Secret Mind of Slime," 2020.

Acknowledgments

How best to capture the movements and moments of grace that accompany the writing of a book? *Yellow* arrived one Saturday morning in October 2020 longhand in a composition book and continued to create its (their) own path. I am indebted to many individuals who helped the flow of *Yellow*'s flourishing.

Primarily, I have Noon Orsatti, muse, to thank and to love for listening to my first nascent chapters, and then as each chapter arrived, becoming fully invested in each character and the world this book created. And where there is Noon, there is his late wife, Pan. Thank you, Bodhisattva.

My other readers include my brother Scott Pence, my friends the Love Supremes John Lebowitz and Margo Barnard, lucid dreamer Jade Rivers, orange Karmann Ghia Katy Silliman and Tim Gerhard. Without you all, I would not have received the inspiration, the fandom, nor the feedback that spurred *Yellow*'s growth. Many thanks to Kaylan Haizlip, who helped me raise some Yellow in her very quiet lab at Pace Academy in 2020 and gave me a new view on science.

My gratitude to writer and poet Jennifer Schomburg Kanke, who read my first draft, was essential in its revisions, and recommended the marvelous writer Claire Bateman to blurb *Yellow*. Thanks to both dwellers from Planet Claire, including the incredible Claire Stanford, whom I met at Hambidge, a place that has supported my work with their residencies.

Many kudos to my agent, Malaga Baldi, who believed in this book and all the wonderful people at Red Hen Press, including Publisher and Executive Director Kate Gale, Monica Fernandez, and Rebeccah Sanhueza. Thanks also to poet, editor, and friend Sandy Meek, who helped me with the last edit.

Thank you artistic collaborators: the talented Teah Charkawi for envisioning Z's doodles and my niece Eleanor Pence for her sketched visions of Yellow. I thank my photographer and daughter Ada Montgomery for her photos, her patience, as well as her exquisite heart.

My many thanks to friends and family. That Pete drifted in a space capsule with the sound of Al Hirt means my stepfather, Bill Newkirk's jazzy piano, and maybe his tunes, accompanied Gemini 5. Another wonder among wonders, traversing our inner and outer space.

Biographical Note

Amy Pence is the author of three poetry collections and two chapbooks, among them *We Travel Towards It*—a work attuned to the personal and collective losses of climate change—and the award-winning hybrid collection *[It] Incandescent*. Her writing spans poetry, interviews, essays, and short fiction. Originally from New Orleans and Las Vegas, she has taught college English and led poetry workshops at Emory University and beyond. She now lives in Atlanta, where she continues to write across genres. *Yellow* is her debut novel. For more, visit amypence.com.